The Last of the
Dream People

293-5833

Books by Alice Anne Parker

Understand Your Dreams:
1500 Basic Dream Images and How to Interpret Them

The Last of the Dream People

THE LAST OF THE
DREAM PEOPLE

Alice Anne Parker

H J KRAMER
TIBURON, CALIFORNIA

H J Kramer Inc
P.O. Box 1082
Tiburon, CA 94920

Editor: Nancy Grimley Carleton
Editorial Assistant: Claudette Charbonneau
Cover Design: Jim Marin/Marin Graphic Services
Cover Photo: Copyright © 1997 by Gerry Ellis/ENP Images.
Composition: Classic Typography

Manufactured in the United States of America.
10 9 8 7 6 5 4 3 2 1

Library of Congress Cataloging-in-Publication Data

Parker, Alice Anne, 1939–
    The last of the dream people / Alice Anne Parker.
        p. cm.
    ISBN 0–915811–79–0
    I. Title.
PS3566.A67474L37   1998
813'.54—dc21   97–37454
                                                                    CIP

To my beloved nephews:

Jack Parker Barnett and Stewart Parker Barnett

It is the mysterious place where all things
begin and end,
where death and birth
pass one into the other.

THE I CHING or BOOK OF CHANGES,
Richard Wilhelm translation

PAPER DOLL WAS GOING DOWN. DENSE SMOKE FILLED THE cockpit. I fought a losing battle with the wheel. "Keep 'er nose up, Kilty." Rusty Cable's voice was in my ear. "Keep 'er nose up." I glanced over at my copilot. His head pitched forward at an impossible angle, left arm hanging uselessly at his side. Then he seemed to raise his head, grinning his cocky grin at me, his freckled face cherubic. He was a happy-go-lucky Van Johnson to my somber Greg Peck. We'd flown together since the beginning. "Got to keep 'er nose up a little longer." I returned to my endless chore, fighting against the ever-increasing force pulling us down, down out of the sky. Fighting my increasing exhaustion.

God only knows where we are. Dense, black, steaming jungle below. We were more than halfway into the run when the ack-ack hit. Little puffs of white smoke far below. It was only a milk run anyway. We didn't expect any action. Didn't even have an escort. Hadn't seen a Nip on this side of the mountains for days. Then we took the hit.

I sent the navigator back to check the damage. He hadn't returned to the cockpit when they hit us again. What is down there, for Christ's sake? The radio was out. Must have gone with the first attack. But someone in the squadron must've seen us turn. Thought we could make it back. Then the second antiaircraft attack ripped through our belly. I turned off course.

Got to find a place to put her down. Can't risk those trees. God, I'm too tired. I can't make it, Rusty. This time he doesn't reply, even in my fevered imagination. A dark, sweetish stench fills the cabin, mixing with the ominous smell of burning insulation. *Holy cow, Rusty, did you crap your pants?*

God, I don't want to die! Not on a milk run, for Christ's sake. This milk wagon is filled with five tons of high-quality explosive and detonating caps that go off if somebody farts loud enough. Too heavy a load. Should only carry four. Too much fuel left in the tanks. Too much high octane fuel to take her down safely.

I risk dropping a hand down to rest for a second on my leg. Something's wrong there, but maybe I don't want to know about it. I'm reassured. My hand feels a leg, and even better, leg feels hand. The nose dips. I drag it back up with both arms, pulling like they're coming out of shoulder sockets. *I can't do it alone. Rusty?*

I must be hallucinating. Some part of me knows he'll never answer again. Still I see him raise his head and look meaningfully in front of the nose. I follow his gaze. Directly ahead of us looms a massive butte, its crown covered with dense, dark green growth, behind it an even higher mountain reaching towards the clouds. I can't get the nose up. We'll never make it over. Then I hear Rusty's voice again. "Take her down now. You can do it, Kilty. Just let her float down. Like a leaf. Take her down easy, real, real easy."

I look where he seems to point. At the foot of the butte, on the left side, a clearing. Too small. Maybe a little longer than a couple of football fields. Way too small. I need close to four thousand feet to put this baby down safely. *Paper Doll* is no slim beauty. She's a deep-bosomed babe loaded with TNT. Maybe I can drop into the slot and coast into the jungle growth at the end. Let the jungle absorb the impact. No choice anyway. Starting to drop now. Slow her down as much as possible. Not enough control. Mustn't stall and drop too soon. Nose up again. Too tired. Arms can't take the punishment. We're going down too fast. Treetops whipping at the undercarriage. Keep the nose up. Fighting against gravity. Fighting the pain.

We drop into the hole and only seconds later impact the green wall at the end of the line.

It's completely dark. I seem to be tied up. Can't move. Can't see. Hot. Burning up. A trickle of cool water in my mouth. There is a fragrance. It is here. Then gone. Pain claims me.

I am awake. Pretending to be asleep. I still can't see. My eyes are covered by something cool. Left arm and shoulder immobile. Right moves a little. Fingers can flex. I feel naked. Still burning. Fingers feel something like a latticework or irregular net wrapped around my torso. Some Jap torture device? It's completely rigid. Yields only slightly when I inflate my lungs to press against it. Hurts to breathe. Ribs broken. I think the thing runs all the way down my left leg. Why can't I raise my right hand? Any movement produces excruciating pain. Dry, sweet smell. Sandalwood. Something tickles a distant memory. I drift off.

I remember sitting in a red booth at a Chinese restaurant on a narrow side street in Seattle, down by the docks. I'm a little kid. Dragons swirl on columns holding up the ceiling. Incense, sandalwood incense. The waiter has a queue. He brings me a few ugly dried-up things arranged on a small red lacquer plate. Gestures that I should put one in my mouth. I'm a bit suspicious, but I pop one in. It is dry, dense, but then I bite into it, releasing a piercing, perfumy juice.

I am given more of them to take home in a rough brown cardboard box. We're driving back to Eugene tonight. My folks are in the front seat of Blackie, our Ford coupe. I fit perfectly on the shelf under the back window. I have a blanket and a pillow. The stars fill the window above me, crisp against the winter sky. The reassuring murmur of voices, my mom and dad speaking softly together. I pop another lichee in my mouth.

The next time I wake up I feel light through my eyelids. I still can't open my eyes. Still pain. Something cool is laid across the lids again. Smells green. The fragrance is present. I am touched very gently here and there by something. A sense of great delicacy. A Chinese nurse? Japs don't have nurses for prisoners of war. Maybe they have other plans for me. Not torture. God, I hope not torture. Maybe they plan to save me for some triumphant public beheading. That's been popular lately. The heads of our men left on stakes for us to find when we take the villages. Medals and dog tags arranged underneath so we can identify the victims. I begin to shudder uncontrollably.

When I wake up again I smell, then feel, the presence of someone. Without thinking I turn my head towards the presence. A very small hand touches me gently on the palm of my right hand. It feels delicate, thin and papery. Then the voice. Dry, whispery. An accent. Asian, but with a slightly British inflection? A trick? Japs are tricky characters. *Be careful. Don't give too much away.*

"Welcome, Captain. I am not reading well, and your papers were singed. You are Captain Ste-ew-art, Keeltee, yes?" The "Stewart" was drawn out into several syllables. "You recover very nice, I think. Not to open eyes yet, please. Eyes okay, I am thinking, but not good yet. There is much pain yet, burns, yes, ribs, right leg, arm bones maybe broken. But good. Good, yes."

I'm not answering. Not yet. I've got to have a plan. I'll pretend ignorance. I'll be grateful for the rescue. Find out as much as I can first. My men? Could any have survived? Where are they? Other huts near here? Need to recover enough to make it through the jungle to our lines. Where the hell are we? How did that character know my nickname? That's not on any of my papers. Find out as much as possible first. Get well. Time to plan an escape. The presence is waiting.

"Drink now, Captain Keeltee. Good drink. You will sleep and dream most important dreams now. Have dreams now. I come back and you tell me your good dreams, yes? We have waited long, longtime for you."

Something cool and slightly acrid is dripped into my mouth.

～ 2 ～

I DON'T KNOW WHAT WAS IN THAT COOL COCKTAIL, BUT I quickly found myself in the most astonishing dream. At first I thought I had wakened up again. I was still in the dark hut, still enmeshed in my stiff lacy net. But this time someone was removing the cool compress from my eyes, and I knew I could open them and see. Kneeling on the mat by my side was a girl of exquisite beauty. Her skin was a glowing golden brown. Fine, waving hair like dark honey cascaded to her waist. She was fine boned, but seemed tall. At first I thought she was half-Tonkinese, one of the exquisite Eurasian girls scattered throughout the Pacific region, but her gaze was too direct. Her eyes were not black, almond-shaped, but golden in the reflected light of the small oil lamp placed beside my mat.

I closed my eyes again. When you're a long way from home, surrounded by men and men only, and maybe you haven't seen a white woman for nineteen months, well, it just works better to put certain things completely out of your mind. Too many guys end up with the heebie-jeebies, or G.I. fever, get sent back to some rock in the middle of the Pacific for R and R, and never make it back to their outfit. I'd learned to discipline my mind, my fantasies, even my dreams. No women for you, Herbert Noone Stewart. No thoughts of women. No dreams of women. I didn't even have photos of women. And I didn't have a girl waiting for me back home.

7

Might have had. Didn't. I opened my eyes again. She was still there.

"Scram," I said weakly.

She shook her head, a grave smile on her face, as the dream began to slowly fade away. I wanted to stop the melting, to make her come back. I raised my right hand in an effort to stop the image dissolving, but as I moved pain engulfed me, drawing me down into searing torment where I tumbled and rolled for the entire restless night.

3

STILL CAN'T OPEN MY EYES. PAIN FLUCTUATING A BIT. MOMENTS of something like clarity. Got to have a plan. Am I a prisoner? Who are my captors? I can't believe the Japs would bother to produce such a complicated plot—and for what possible purpose? Who was that girl? Maybe I wasn't dreaming last night. That drink might have been a drug. I was drugged and she appeared.

The light in the hut changed. Someone had entered. The feeling of presence strong. The dry, woodsy fragrance.

"Good morning, Keeltee. Not so good last night? Still big pain today. Good dream comes like gift. Next time take gift, yes?"

I raised my head to speak, instantly thought better of it, and dropped it back to the mat.

"Drink first. Eat. Then time for talk." The presence held something up to my lips. A stiff leaf folded into cup shape. I gulped the cool water down and opened my mouth for more. When my thirst was quenched the cup was presented to me again. This time it was filled with a sweet pastelike substance that tasted like sweet potatoes, banana, and oatmeal mush. I gulped it down and nodded for more.

"Good, Keeltee. Better now. I check eyes and we talk some, yes. Keeping eyes closed first, yes?"

I nodded as the delicate but surprisingly strong hands raised my head, placing some kind of firm bolster under my head and shoulders. Then the cool dressing was carefully removed and something was smeared over my lids. Behind my closed eyes I felt the light darken.

"Good, Keeltee. Open eyes now. Slow. Slow."

With great difficulty I managed to raise my lids. Everything was dark gray. I frowned.

"Not to worry, now. Here is light on left. Watch now. Seeing light on left?"

A flicker on my left shifted the intensity of the darkness. I nodded.

"Now on right? Seeing light on right?"

Again I nodded.

"Good. Good. Eyes must stay quiet now. Rest eyes and we talk." More of something cool was smeared on my closed lids, and a new dressing placed there.

"So? You have many questions."

I nodded. "My men. Are any others here? What happened to the plane? How did you get me out?"

"All dead. Completely, finally, dead forever. You only part dead. No others here. Burning in cockpit. We put fire out. Drain fuel tank. Better no fire."

I puzzled for a moment. "I don't understand. How far are we from the plane? Can you take me there soon? Why did you drain the tanks?" I believed him. Some part of me already knew the others were dead, but another part couldn't quite accept it. I had to see it. I had to know exactly what had happened to *Paper Doll*.

"Captain Keeltee, Japoni too close now. We drain tanks so no fire. We cover plane with branches, leaves. Putting one man in your chair. Your necklace on him. When Japoni come all dead. Captain Keeltee dead too. No petrol. No searching." The voice was silent for a moment, then continued. "Cannot go there. Others will come, maybe tonight, talk with you. They go home now. Better. It is good now. No problem."

I couldn't follow him. What others were coming? Who was going home? I tried again. "Who are you? What others are you talking about? Where am I? You said you were waiting for me. What do you mean?"

Suddenly I was exhausted. I shook my head and feebly raised my one good hand. He got the message.

"Okay, Keeltee. Sleep now. Take one piss first, yes?" He gently moved my penis so that it rested in the neck of some vessel. With considerable difficulty and great relief I eventually managed to pee for quite a long time.

When I woke again the presence was waiting. It smelled like night. Again I drank, ate, pissed. He removed the dressing and suggested I open my eyes. In the gray now some shapes moved. I could discern a form where he sat, next to my mat.

"Talk more, yes. Not too much. You are strong. Good. We must move soon. Others go home now. Maybe they talk to you tonight, yes?"

I couldn't follow this. I tried again. "Who are you? What others? You said my men were dead. Where am I? Are you Chinese? You said you were waiting for me. What do you mean?"

The presence rested his small, dry hand in mine again. The fingers gently tapped my palm a few times as if he were considering my questions. Then he laughed, a little high-pitched, tinkling sound. "I am Uda. Not Chinese, oh no. Many years ago I hear you are coming. Speaking English. I have gone to English hospital. Longtime walk and walk. One must go to learn English, yes? Then, short time, I see you are coming soon. I walk, walk, come back. I am waiting when you come. Plane comes. We grab you out, quick, quick, only a little dead."

I must be feverish. Maybe this is all a fever dream. The pain seems real enough. When I say nothing in response Uda taps my palm again a few times as if to gain my attention. "Drink now, Keeltee. Have good dreams now. Good dream like gift. Take gift tonight, yes?"

The cool, acrid liquid is held up to my mouth. I drink it all.

4

IT SEEMED I ONLY CLOSED MY EYES FOR A FEW SECONDS.
I opened them again to find myself still in the dimly lit hut,
but able to see perfectly well. Once again the beautiful young
woman knelt by my mat, the flickering oil lamp next to her.

I looked directly into her eyes, and she held my gaze.
Something began to happen to me—like being out in the
waves on the coast and looking up to see the big roller coming. You want to start swimming madly for the shore, but
you know you have to dive, to get under it, to come up on
the other side. I couldn't hold her gaze. I closed my eyes.
Then in a moment of quick panic—what if she was gone?—
they flew open again.

She was there. I looked directly at her again. Easier this
time. Not so much undertow to fight against. She smiled, just
a little, then began gently unwrapping the green lattice that
held my broken limbs together. I protested. "Look," I said,
"I don't think those should come off yet. . . . I . . . ."

She stopped her work and looked directly into my eyes.
It was easier this time. I didn't fight the wave at all. She didn't
speak out loud, but I heard her voice inside my head or something. She reminded me that I was dreaming. This made
sense to me. Not to worry. It was only a dream. She told me
that she had come to heal me while I was asleep. She told
me that she had been waiting a long, longtime for me to come,

13

but that time was now short and I must heal as quickly as possible since we would be moving soon. She said she would work with me every night so I would get better faster. She said her name was Anjang.

All this was just too darn much for me. All my discipline went straight to hell as soon as I felt the touch of her strong, cool hands. I moaned a couple of times and then just gave up completely. Wherever she laid those cool hands the pain started slowly, mercifully, to drain away.

The girl would take a small amount of something like milky jelly from a coconut half filled with the slippery stuff, hold it in both hands up to her face, and breathe softly into it with her eyes closed. She whispered a kind of incantation in a language I couldn't understand. Then she massaged me with the jelly, while chanting in a low, musical voice. She began at my forehead, deftly smoothing the cool stuff over the painful blisters that were oozing liquid as they healed.

By the time she reached my belly I was nervous. An ominous twitching from my groin now accompanied her skilled massage. At least my cock was hidden in the shadows. To my consternation she seemed to hear my thoughts. She smiled a little and quickly turned to look where I was most afraid she would look, and, at the same time, most feared she wouldn't. I groaned as she deftly cupped my testicles in a careful hand. Then to my complete horror, she gave a little gasp and dropped them.

"Your member! There is damage here!"

Was it burned beyond recognition? It couldn't be, could it? I would feel it. But maybe it was like those fellows who lost a limb and then went completely nuts trying to scratch something that wasn't there. Maybe you could feel an erection after serious damage even when there wasn't anything left to get hard.

In the dream I was able to raise myself to enough of a sitting position so I could see my cock. Relief swept over me, and I fell back down, panting from the sudden exertion. It was okay. Nothing to boast about—I wasn't one of those guys who worshipped his manhood—but it was all there, pink and proud.

I guess I spoke out loud. "That's it. It's all there. Thank God, it's all there."

She reached down and carefully cradled my erection in both hands. To my great embarrassment, I came.

Now the dream changed. I don't know if it was the combination of shame and embarrassment I was feeling or what, but I was no longer in the hut with graceful Anjang. Instead, I found myself in a room in the Dan Moore Hotel in Portland, Oregon, poised over the sweaty little body of someone whose name I couldn't remember, if I ever knew it in the first place. I was a senior in high school, and it was the night before the final game of the state high school basketball tournament. Tomorrow we would play our traditional rival, Beaverton High, for first place.

We proud Eugene High School Axemen had pooled our resources and sent one of our first string guards, Binky Druitt, to find some willing girls. He drove to a seedy joint on the coast road called the Chicken Shack, where he enticed a couple of pullets from Mollala to join the team at the hotel.

We weren't fortified by alcohol. Coach Kuchara would kill us if we broke training by drinking the night before the big game. I guess I was number five. We waited our turns in

15

an adjoining room while our team members worked out on the girls on the two beds next door.

I hated the memory of that night. Hated the recurring dream that grew more squalid with each repetition. Hated her face when I looked down at her under me. Eyebrows growing almost together. Eyes squeezed shut. Then she opened her eyes and looked at me. Little eyes, pink-rimmed, pale lashes. I hadn't done anything yet. Her eyes held such pain, such a bottomless well of pain and misery and loathing, of herself, of me, even of basketball, I imagine. I didn't even get it in. I saw the misery in her eyes. I came.

She gave a grunt of disgust and rolled me off of her onto the floor, wiping at her stomach. It was my first time with a girl.

We lost the game the next day. It wasn't really that important to me. We were going to be in a war any day now. That seemed more important than a basketball game. Binky said he'd rather have a whore than another trophy anyway.

I slid away from the old nightmare, back into the earlier dream in the hut. When I opened my eyes again, Anjang was there, gazing at me with a look of deep sympathy. She touched my penis again, gently, carefully.

"How wounded here?"

I frowned, confused by her comment. I think I still heard her words in my head. Or maybe we spoke out loud. Sometimes even when I'm awake I can't tell anymore.

"I'm not wounded there. That's how it is. Are men here different?"

She was clearly puzzled now. She leaned down closer and carefully examined my organ, tracing the raised scar tissue a few inches below the head of the penis. "Apron is missing. Men have apron here. Protects softness there." As she spoke she gently followed the scar with the tip of one finger, then touched the end of my penis.

Of course. How dumb can you get? I was circumcised right after I was born, just like everyone else I knew. Except that one guy. Buzzy Wicks. An Arkie who arrived in Eugene our junior year in high school. Took a lot of ribbing from the other guys in the showers after P.E. class. This must be some primitive tribe, isolated in the jungle since time began. Maybe never exposed to any civilization. Except how did she speak English? I put that question aside for the moment.

"I'm circumcised. It's a medical thing. In America boy babies have their foreskins—their aprons—removed right after birth. It doesn't hurt. At least I don't remember it. It's quite a good thing. We do it for . . ." I had to think for a minute. Hygiene wasn't it? Something disgusting would happen otherwise. But this beautiful, this incredibly, exotically beautiful woman wasn't looking at me or listening. She had taken my penis again in her two hands and was crooning over it the way I'd seen a mother croon over a crying baby with a bellyache. Then she leaned down and took my penis into her mouth, gently caressing the scar with her tongue. I melted away. After only a little of this, I came again.

5

THE NEXT MORNING I FELT LIKE A COMPLETELY DIFFERENT person. I knew I ought to think things through carefully, but mostly I felt elated and oddly carefree. My pain was back, but nothing like the torture of the first couple of days. I knew I was pretty badly hurt, but the pain floated somewhere outside of me instead of requiring most of my energy to bear. I could think about something else for the first time since the crash. My problem was, all I wanted to think about was the night before.

Nothing seemed completely real, or made much sense to me. I remembered that the presence with the light, dry fragrance was named Uda. The dream woman was Anjang. I pigeonholed these facts in my mind, as if I could anchor to them. It may seem odd that I didn't further question the truth of Anjang's existence. But I didn't. From that second visit she became as important to me as anything that has ever happened to me before or since, asleep or awake.

But how did we talk? Uda said he had learned English because I was coming and I spoke English. Was that right? How did I talk to Anjang? She said I had to recover fast because we needed to move. I did move, didn't I? I sat up, moved arms and legs around under my own steam. I came. Then I came again. That part was real. A wonderful lightness around my groin, not to mention in my spirit, confirmed that.

The light in my hut changed. Someone had entered. A strong feeling of presence. The dry, woodsy fragrance.

"Anjang?" I couldn't keep a note of hopeful expectation out of my voice. I heard the high tinkle of laughter again.

"Good morning, Keeltee. Sleep good? Good dreaming, yes? Very good dreaming, I think. Good healing, yes? Today bright."

I sure didn't want to discuss my sex life, even my dream sex life, with an invisible stranger. I ignored the comments, not questioning the fact that Uda seemed to have detailed intelligence of my activities during the night. It was time for me to get some answers to my questions.

∼ 6 ∼

THREE OR FOUR MORE DAYS PASSED IN PRETTY MUCH THE same way. I slept and woke up, each time finding Uda or a young boy, who called himself B'ma, waiting. I drank, ate, pissed, and shat, asked more questions, tried to make some sense of the answers, slept again. Each time I woke my eyes improved. Each time I slept I dreamed again of Anjang, who massaged me, holding my penis and crooning over it. She seemed pleased with the progress of my recovery, but when I attempted to sit up, to caress, or to embrace her, she only shook her head. Again she told me we must move soon.

Why doesn't she come to my hut when I am awake? I will question Uda about this.

I am lying on a woven mat in a small, oval hut constructed of saplings woven together and roughly covered by thick, heart-shaped leaves. It's hot during the day, humid, but not oppressive. The temperature drops when the sun goes down. At night the boy covers me with a kind of blanket made from something like soft, thick paper. Mosquitoes trouble me a little during the day, although they disappear when it cools down in the evening and the breeze comes up. I'm concerned about getting malaria or dengue fever. Doesn't seem likely I can get quinine here.

Uda must be a tribal elder or maybe the chief. He has the strangest eyes. Like Anjang's, they're almost golden. His face is small, quite childlike, although deeply wrinkled and lined, huge ears, enormous ears, actually, and round eyes slit across the middle, like a turtle. In fact, he looks quite a bit like a wise old turtle.

⌦

Oct. 11, 1944 (uncertain about this date, I don't know how long I was unconscious after *Paper Doll* crashed)

I have prevailed upon Uda to send a party to reconnoiter *Paper Doll*. They returned safely with my dispatch case and a box of detonators—which may prove invaluable if what I am beginning to suspect is true. I'm starting a record of events. Can't see well enough yet to write much.

Oct. 14, 1944

The papers I was carrying that could prove interesting to our enemies and dangerous to our forces in the field have now been destroyed. I will endeavor to preserve an account of my experiences in this journal, for I am beginning to think something very strange is happening here. If I do not survive this experience and this journal is found, please send it to my commanding officer: Lt. Col. Roger Bluett, USAAF, 5th Air Force; or to my parents: John and Alice Stewart, 2089 Potter St., Eugene, Ore., USA. I am Captain Herbert Noone Stewart, #0-361461. My identity tags have been left in the wreckage of my plane on the body of one of my crew members.

Oct. 15, 1944

As to my situation here: I am in the care of a friendly local tribe, who appear to have a hostile relationship towards the Japanese invaders. Due to my condition (probable broken ribs, leg, burns, extensive bruising), I have had contact with only one adult, Uda, who may be a headman, and with a young boy.

After lengthy questioning of Uda, I have deduced the following: Some distant generation, not Uda's father or mother or their parents, or even theirs, or theirs—more than ten generations ago, by his reckoning—a member of his family had a "great, great" dream.

A long parenthesis here: The importance of dreams to this tribe (who call themselves "the people of the dream world" or "the people of the dream") is virtually without limit—something like the American Bill of Rights and the New Testament combined. For them authority rests primarily in dreams. For example, "great dreams" come to keep someone on track as to his or her life's direction, while "great, great dreams" have meaning for the whole group, to a destiny that all members of the tribe share.

Great, great dreams used to be rare; in the past, years would go by without any at all. However, as this so-called "destiny" nears completion, if I understand Uda correctly, great, great dreams become more common. A number of people can have great, great dreams at the same time, although with slight variations. Additional details from these individual dreams contribute to the complete dream message. Uda added that children are frequently the ones who have great, great dreams, and oftentimes a child's special gifts are recognized when he or she has received a great, great dream.

Oct. 16, 1944

Today with some effort I can sit up by myself. Uda says the light outside the hut is still too bright for my eyes. B'ma stays with me whenever I'm awake—tends to my needs. He must be nine or ten. Captivating face with delicate, even features. Honey brown skin similar to Anjang's, but a little darker, like light molasses. Doesn't speak any English. Several others I haven't seen yet, although I hear their voices outside the hut. Where is Anjang? When I ask Uda, he just says, "She will come tonight."

Now here is the part that is so strange that I am almost hesitant to preserve it on paper. Although writing something in a loose-leaf notebook with a pencil in the middle of a tropical jungle God-knows-where is somewhat of a joke as far as preservation goes. But here it is. Uda's distant ancestor dreamed that a "messenger" would descend from the skies. That seems to be the gist of it initially. However, as far as I understand it, the details of this coming visitation have accumulated over the years. So much so that Uda himself, while still a young person, learned in a dream that he must go many miles away to learn the language that would be spoken by "the messenger." Sometime later he left on a journey that took a "long, longtime," apparently a greater distance than one taking only a "longtime." When he eventually reached a clinic staffed by a British doctor and several nurses—or maybe a priest and nuns, I couldn't be sure from his description—he recognized the language that had been spoken in the dream and stayed there for a number of years to learn it.

In general these people seem to have only four numbers: one, two, three, and many. Uda is proud of his ability to count higher than three, but after ten his figures become somewhat arbitrary. He told me he stayed at the clinic for "twenty" or maybe "eleven" years.

Later the same day:

I should add that as far as I can determine, Uda is the first and only member of his tribe to have had any contact with the outside world. Until I arrived, of course.

Even stranger. Some time ago Uda learned from another dream that he must return to the tribe and be ready to welcome the "sooncome messenger." In brief he said to me, "I walk, walk, come back. Here you are." I protested that I had no reason to believe that I was the expected messenger. He assured me that I was and that he could prove it. When I doubted him he triumphantly announced that my name was all the evidence needed. I have been nicknamed Kilty since I was about five years old, for reasons that I'm too weary to explain just now. "Keeltee," as Uda pronounces my name, is the term in their language for "messenger," "message," and "good news."

～ 7 ～

Oct. 18, 1944

Very bad dream last night. I am with Anjang in the hut, enjoying my nightly session of healing massage, when there are noises outside. I hear shots, followed by yelling, and terrible screams. Anjang races out. I follow more slowly. It is very dark at first. Then I see a scene of the most hideous violence. Five men and B'ma have been slaughtered around the small campfire that burns continuously outside the hut. One of the men, whom I recognize as Uda, has an arrow in his throat and may still be alive. Two of the men have been shot in the chest. The other two and B'ma have their throats cut. Blood is everywhere. Anjang is gone. I fall to the ground and begin screaming in a hideous voice—like a calf being slaughtered.

I am awakened by Uda, who has raced to the hut at the sound of my yelling. When I tell him I have had a violent nightmare he becomes very serious and insists I repeat every detail to him over and over again. He is interested in my description of the other four men, whom I have yet to see when awake. I describe them thusly: Two are tall and slender, although muscular. They have golden brown skin like Anjang's and B'ma's, but darker, although not so dark as the third man. These two appear to be brothers, maybe even twins—I am guessing here. They have handsome features, narrow noses, large eyes, and fine high foreheads. Both have dense curly hair, cropped short, of a medium brown. The third man is stockier and darker in color, with powerful shoulders and heavily muscled legs. His nose is broader, and his head is much rounder. The fourth man is also taller. He has long arms and a wide mouth. I want to say that he is very humorous, although I have no way of knowing this. Nevertheless, I mention my observation to Uda and he nods encouragement, asking me to close my eyes and explore the scene attentively, looking for additional details.

Uda questions me carefully about the arrow. I am afraid I am disappointing him as I cannot with any accuracy describe whether it is fletched with feathers or decorated in any other way.

When Uda has extracted all possible information from me, he sits for a moment with his eyes closed. He opens them and smiles, although I sense concern on his part. "Very good dreaming, Keel-tee. You learning quick, quick. Tomorrow we go." Without another word he slips out of the hut, apparently to wake the others.

⁌⁍

It is now morning. I am sitting under a makeshift shelter outside, watching the preparations for our journey and writing in my journal. In front of me, to my considerable astonishment, the very same four men I saw in my dream are working away. Ete and Sua, the two brothers (I was correct in my guess) are building a kind of hammock or sling, in which I will be carried, something like a large hog. They are fashioning a netlike contrivance from some pliable vines, which have been stripped of leaves by B'ma. The brothers appear to be about my age—early twenties, I should say. The very muscular older man, Heeta, has just returned from an expedition with Masamo, the taller of the two, the one with the wide mouth. Indeed, he is always laughing and greets me with a wide smile every time I look up from my writing. I believe they have been constructing some sort of booby trap on the trail below, as there was much discussion and drawing of plans with sticks in the dirt before their departure early this morning.

Uda has told me we will leave at dusk. If I understand him correctly there is a dangerous passageway along a narrow cliff, during which we will be exposed to the view of any watchers below. By traversing this passage in the dark, we will avoid detection. It will be best if I sleep, he has said, as my eyes and ears will be of little use. I believe he has told me that I can help them best by dreaming. Last night's evidence to the contrary, I would hesitate to trust my life to such an unreliable source of intelligence.

Uda sits beside me, under the shade of a kind of leafy verandah, which was created in the most expeditious way by the simple process of drawing the tops of four saplings together, tying them with a length of vine a few feet from the top, and then spreading the leaves. I have had my casts redone this morning, and am much more comfortable, as only my lower right leg and left shoulder are now encased in the stiff netting. Uda has warned me to keep my left arm still, and it is loosely bound against my chest. I haven't been allowed to hop around, but I believe I could get around with a crutch if it became necessary. I am still in some pain, especially when I move or bump against anything.

It's great to be outside finally. I know we're in a hurry, and we seem to be in serious danger, but I can't help feeling a kind of reckless joy. This is odd, even confusing. As immediately as I feel this wave of soaring excitement, I'm struck by an equally vast feeling of loss. The men I have been closer to than almost anyone else in my life are dead. I'd give almost anything for a quart of scotch. Then I could express my grief in the time-honored way of getting totally, blindly, helplessly drunk.

When I look up from my writing, Uda is regarding me with his deep, gentle eyes. I am tempted to believe that he senses almost everything that I feel. No doubt it is the total isolation from everything familiar to me, plus the shock, physical and mental, I have recently experienced, that leads me to such romantic fantasy.

Uda is making a rope. B'ma has fetched a quantity of stringy vine, which Uda strips and softens by pulling through the cleft between his thumb and forefinger. He then rapidly and deftly twists it into a strong cord, coiling it into lengths of at least one hundred feet. He wears a kind of wrapper which encases his body from the armpits to mid-calf. It may be fabric, or more likely, a kind of tapa cloth like the stuff I have seen made by the Polynesian natives. The others wear only a string around the waist, with a long piece of soft, barklike material that runs between the legs, hanging over the string in front and back. I have been provided with a similar outfit. I guess you could call it a jungle jockstrap.

Anjang is not here. Has never been here. Uda tells me that she and the rest of their small group are far away (but not far, far away!). It seems we will have a journey of more than three days (but not many) to reach them, although I can't be sure, as I think we will often travel by night and sleep by day.

A funny story. Uda has told me before that they are "the people of the dream," or "the people of the dream world." Sometimes if I ask why something is done a certain way, or the reason for a particular practice, he will answer, "Because we are people of the dream," which he seems to think explains all! Today, as he worked on the rope, I asked him what the word for his tribe was in their own language. At first he didn't understand the question, but eventually replied with a word that sounded like "S'norra," then pointed towards the sky and said something like "S'norr," very loud, with a rolled "r" and a rasping sound. I asked him to repeat this and he did so even louder, sounding like nothing so much as someone sleeping with his mouth open after Sunday dinner. I guess it really tickled me, because when I put this sound together with the notion of them being "the dream people," I fell into quite a gale of laughing until I was almost choking from hiccups. Uda laughed a little along with me, quite politely. When I had recovered from my fit of hilarity, he asked to be let in on the joke. Well, you can imagine what a time I had explaining it! I eventually succeeded by acting out the Sunday sleeper, making a great snoring sound.

Then Uda got the joke. He shrieked like a stuck pig, throwing himself flat on his back and kicking into the air with both legs, while the others regarded him with apparent envy. Now he had to explain the joke to them, but his explanation kept being interrupted by further fits of laughing. I have to say that I got the bug again and laughed at his laughter until tears rolled down my face. When Uda finally got the joke across, everyone joined the fun, slapping themselves on their round bellies and snapping their fingers with delight.

This has become a great joke between us now, and even the tiniest snorelike sound will cause a fit of hilarity to radiate through the entire group.

Another funny thing. B'ma hangs on my every word, and is especially interested when I use any slang. He has formed the habit of shouting "holy cow" at every opportunity. When he asked Uda to explain the meaning of the term, and Uda asked me, I was at a complete loss. What does "holy cow" mean, for gosh sakes? I am being careful not to use more serious profanity in B'ma's presence. I tried to explain to Uda about swearing. I acted out someone hitting his thumb with a hammer and then cursing at the pain as an example. Uda then pretended to stub his toe on an exposed root. He jumped around and made an "ssssss" sound but didn't say any words. They apparently have no profanity of any kind in their language. I'm not sure I explained what profanity really was, anyway. Maybe I don't actually know.

Our camp is on a small plateau, a bit less than an acre in size, jutting out about a third of the way up the great butte. As I sit here I am constantly drawn to gaze out on the vista spread below. A vast, dense jungle stretches as far as I can see in three directions, with a distant ridge on the west, to my left. Silver threads of stream glitter here and there, catching the light as the sun breaks through the clouds moving above. There is no evidence of human settlement, no encampment, no roads of any sort. I deeply regret the loss of our charts in the cockpit fire. I am sure I could pinpoint our location from this vantage point it they had been saved.

Uda is making fun of me. When I remark to him on the absence of people below, he loses no time in correcting my error. He points out two barely visible coils of smoke marking enemy camps. In other places a slight change in the dense black green of the jungle indicates areas where trees have been cleared for planting. Uda assures me that the country below is fairly crawling with population. As he describes it, it is like a crowded city compared to the relatively under-populated highlands where his people live. It is true, of course, that his idea of a crowded place is probably a tiny hamlet of forty souls.

He has explained to me that my dream indicates we are in imminent danger from three different groups, all traditional or present enemies of the S'norra.

As I understand him, the native population below is now in the pocket of the Japanese invaders, who have armed the local tribes with modern weapons, including high-powered rifles. In the past, the S'norra have efficiently held off any attempts from the lowlanders to oust them from their territory. However their blowguns and bows and arrows are no match for modern weaponry, and they have been forced to retreat to higher and higher ground. He says only "some" people are left of his tribe that once numbered "many" groups of "many" people.

In my dream the men were killed in three different ways: Two were shot, one was hit with a bow and arrow, two had their throats cut. Uda says this indicates we are in danger from two different tribes, plus the Japanese; the tribe he calls "the animals," who now use guns, and "the fools," who still use bows and arrows. He adds that only the Japanese are insane enough to cut the throat of a young boy. He mentions in a seemingly offhand way that "the animals" and "the fools" have probably told the Japanese of the secret knowledge held by the S'norra. However, now that the messenger has arrived the S'norra have nothing to fear. This last line is delivered with a significant look in my direction. He then repeats the line in S'norran to the others, who turn to me with looks of considerable devotion and murmur something approvingly. I am at a complete loss. Is it possible that I have been brought here by some divine providence to save these people from the Japanese invaders? How in the hell am I going to do that?

8

Oct. 19, 1944

Late afternoon. Everyone naps except me and Masamo, who is keeping watch over the trail below. Quite a hair-raising night. First I was loaded into my hammock, while the four men raised the bamboo poles to their shoulders, all groaning and protesting at the huge weight. Then they raced around with me at a great speed, making quite a show of their strength and agility. Next the whole package was unceremoniously dumped on the ground, me still inside, while some debate raged as to whether or not I was to be sewn up inside the hammock. My opinion was not consulted, although once I had determined the subject of the debate you can bet I protested. Consequently I was not sewn inside.

I should add that I am six feet two inches tall in my stocking feet and tip the scales at one hundred and eighty-seven pounds stripped. At least that's what I weighed ten days ago. I have noted here that Masamo is the taller of the men. I would guess him to be five foot five or six, while the others are smaller. In addition to hauling me, each of the men is carrying on his back a deep basket, loaded with provisions, the whole thing secured by a kind of tumpline which stretches across the neck and shoulders. Two are armed with bow and arrows. The others have blowguns slung on their shoulders, plus a hanging gourd which contains poison and darts. The detonators have been wrapped in leaves, after being carefully cushioned with thick pads of moss. Uda carries them in his basket.

Two of the other men carry live coals, which they packaged very neatly in damp leaves. I have my journal and two precious pencils, carefully wrapped in large leaves and bound with cord, tied into the hammock next to me. I am to keep my knees bent whenever possible, making it easier for my bearers to round some of the tight curves on the trail.

Feeling like Gulliver bound and trussed by the Lilliputians, I breathed a prayer to whatever gods were watching over us and we set out. After a short time it was fully dark and we stopped for a rest. Uda approached me with a leaf cup containing some of the evening cocktail I have become accustomed to drinking at night. It had occurred to me that I might prefer to be conscious, given the perils of our journey, but Uda was insistent. I finally took a few swallows, but less than usual. Nevertheless, in a very short time I fell asleep.

Sometime later I gradually drifted into consciousness. Above me was a glorious display of stars, strangely arranged. The few constellations I recognized were in the wrong position; other star groups were completely unfamiliar. I seemed to be rocking gently in my hammock, suspended in a black, velvety space with only the glittering stars above. I was reminded of my cozy nest in Blackie, my folks' Ford coupe. Some distance away I could hear murmuring voices. I felt wonderfully secure, perfectly comfortable, and I began to drift back into sleep. Then I gave a sudden start and jerked completely awake. Where were my bearers? I was hanging in space on the face of a massive cliff! I twisted my neck around to look down. Nothing. I gave a yelp and struggled to rise. I was sewn into my hammock after all. Now I was really browned off, and I let off a roar of fear and anger. Uda's head popped over the edge of the cliff some distance above me. "Keeltee!" His voice was quietly urgent. "No problem, Keeltee, coming up now. Quiet. Quiet."

Inch by inch I was dragged up the face of the cliff. Now I knew the purpose of those ropes Uda had woven. After what seemed hours, although I imagine it was no more than fifteen minutes, I was pulled over the cliff edge onto a narrow, flat ledge, where a makeshift pulley had been rigged around a massive boulder. I was royally steamed, you can bet. No one stepped forward to cut loose the binding for a bit. Then B'ma was sent to me with one of the sharpened flints they use as knives to cut the vines holding me in. With as much dignity as I could muster, I managed to pull myself to a sitting position. The others sat a short distance away, sharing some food that had been wrapped in leaves and packed in one of the baskets. No one looked in my direction.

After a while one of the men made a snoring sound and the others giggled, glancing over at me to see if I would laugh. I turned my head away and gazed out at the stars. A short time later Uda came to me, ignoring completely my childish temper. He handed me a packet of food and patted me on the shoulder. "Good, Keeltee." Oddly enough I felt tears spring to my eyes when he patted me. I felt I had behaved badly and had been generously forgiven.

We traveled along a narrow cliff edge for the rest of the night. At times when I caught a glimpse of the sheer drop below I almost wished I was still asleep.

We're still quite a ways from the summit of the butte. I imagine we will travel again when it is dusk.

Oct. 21, 1944

We have stopped to rest on a wide ledge. Everyone sleeps except for me and Heeta, who lies on his belly close to the edge, head poised to watch the trail below us. Uda says we will continue until just before dawn, by which time we will have reached "a good place," where we will spend a day or so to rest and replenish our stock of food. He also says he thinks we are being trailed by "the animals," as they are noisy and clumsy (by which I assume he means physically larger than the S'norra). Masamo—he's the kidder—acts out their stumbling movements to the delight of the others. When Uda remarks that "the animals" are, however, armed with Arisakas, Japanese high-powered rifles, everyone becomes immediately serious. We seem to have made our way completely around the face of the butte. If my calculations are correct, the wall behind me is to the north. We are now facing out towards the south. I am trying to keep directions straight in my head, tough to do in the dark, especially as the trail constantly curves around the butte and then doubles back on itself. There are other trails that fork off, and we don't always take the main route. I have noticed that there is no discussion at these junctions—all seem agreed in advance on which path to take. I will try to make a rough map of our route when we stop at the good place.

9

WE REACHED THE GOOD PLACE SHORTLY BEFORE DAWN AS
Uda had predicted. It is beautiful beyond any imagining. I
should be working on my map. Instead, I sit by a deep pool
of clear, cool water, trying to comprehend what is going on.
I've been talking to Uda about mining the trail behind us
with a couple of the detonators. I carefully explained possible ways to rig the blast. As he didn't seem to understand, I
explained again in different terms. He listened to my description of what the results would be when one of "the animals"
tripped the mechanism.

"Keeltee," he finally asked, "would kill the animals behind
us, yes?"

"Kill, maim, damage—definitely. Might take most of the
trail out with them. Is that a problem?"

He looked away for some time, his face extremely thoughtful. Finally he turned back to me.

"Keeltee, why kill the animals?"

I was completely flummoxed by this question, you can
believe.

"They're af-after us!" I finally managed to stutter. "Isn't
that why we're running? What about my dream? I thought
my dream was a warning. You said . . . Anjang said . . . you
both said we had to move soon. Aren't they following us?
Don't we need to get away?"

Again there was a long silence. Uda sniffed the breeze, watched a bird moving across the clearing where we sat, not hopping as birds everywhere else in the world do, but walking on stiff, bright yellow legs, turning its head curiously this way and that. Finally, he answered: "We run from animals, yes, but we run because if animals catch us we must kill them. No need to kill animals. Cannot eat them."

Only a few days ago I was dropping bombs on people I had never seen; now I'm busting my ass to get away from savages because if they catch us we'll have to kill them! Something about the logic of this escapes me. It sure makes a cocked hat out of my assumption that I need to protect the S'norra from their enemies. I just can't make the whole thing out at all.

Uda, for once, seems indifferent to my feelings. He is sitting next to me on a rocky outcropping alongside the water. This place reminds me of the pool where Tarzan first meets Jane. I keep imagining that Anjang is reclining on the bank on the other side, and I dive in and swim over to her—you get the picture. In my fantasy, of course, no one else is around. Except for Cheeta.

I guess Tarzan movies are still my major source of information about jungles—and natives. It's funny, I've been flying over jungles for almost a year, but this is the first time I've actually been right in the heart of one.

To describe this place as a jungle is inadequate anyway. I'd call it paradise. Rising above us is a magnificent mountain peak with knife-edge ridges, covered with velvety dark green vegetation. I take it that's where we're heading in a few days. It's very different from the granite mountains of the

Cascades in Oregon. They're beautiful, of course, but austere, challenging—somehow you feel compelled to measure yourself against them. This peak looks inviting, soft, welcoming. In the early morning, right after we first arrived, the peak was still shrouded in mist. We sat together, resting, while we watched the mist began to break up, dissolving like wisps of smoke until eventually the entire peak was revealed. It was a pretty amazing sight. I asked Uda if the mountain has a name. He told me that it doesn't have a name, but that it is "the way home." Then a bit later, he added that it is also "destiny mountain," or "death mountain."

While I contemplate his answer, he waits peacefully. Then he turns to me again and explains that there is one word in S'norran (something quite unpronounceable) which means "the way home," "destiny," but also "death." He added that any time he uses one of these terms, either of the other two words could be substituted in its place.

I am drying off in the sun after a long, refreshing swim in this cool, clean water. Uda said I was ready to exercise my limbs, so my hammock was lowered into the water until I was submerged and could roll out. Mostly I just floated around, but it did feel swell to have my weight completely supported by the water. Getting me out was a different matter—the problem was finally solved by lowering my hammock again until I could roll back into it and be dragged out. My latticework casts grew soft in the water and are now stiffening again as they dry in the sun. I'll be glad to have them off completely. Uda says soon.

Everyone except for Masamo and Uda left on a foraging expedition right after we arrived. When they returned, Heeta carried a monkey carcass, killed with bow and arrow; Sua's hands were filled with some fluffy pink and gray mushrooms; and Ete had a package wrapped in green leaves which he carried like a precious treasure. On inspection it proved to be a honeycomb, dripping with amber honey and filled with grubs and larvae. This was immediately dropped into a pot with some water and placed over the small fire to soften. We shared a remarkable lunch of honey water and chewy grubs, some still alive. I guess dinner will consist of monkey meat with mushroom stew! It's a change from our standard chow of sweet potato and banana mush. As I recover my strength, I am also recovering my appetite. I'm hungry all the time. The others watch me eat with amazement. They haven't seen anything yet. What I wouldn't give for a big plate of bacon and eggs—with hot coffee and buttered toast. Or steak. Wild blackberry pie. Cold milk. Or cold beer. An ice cold Olympia.

While I was having my dip the whole gang piled in the water. It was really something to watch the twins, Ete and Sua, whooping and swinging across on vines before they launched themselves into the drink. Johnny Weismuller doesn't have anything on these guys for jungle acrobatics. Uda climbed to the top of the rocks—there's a little falls that drops about twelve feet into the deep pool—and then stood at the top, a total lack of expression on his face. I watched him a bit worriedly from where I was floating on one side, avoiding the traffic—it's clear he's quite a bit older than the others. I wondered if he didn't approve of the high jinks. Then when everyone was finally quiet and looking up at him, he did a dead man fall from the top of the rocks into the water, not even raising his arms. I was scared for a minute, to tell the truth, but the others shrieked with laughter, so I guess it was a great joke. He did a stately breast stroke to the edge of the pool and climbed out. What to make of that? It's like he made a joke out of his own dignity.

I'd been thinking about what he said earlier, about not killing "the animals." So I asked him if the S'norra thought that killing was a sin. He sucked in his cheeks and narrowed his eyes so that just a small band of light showed—this is a common facial expression for him. He answered me, "No, no sin—sometimes necessary, but best to avoid. Killing means bad dreams."

I should have left it there. Instead I said something foolish about the Ten Commandments and how "Thou shalt not kill" was of necessity suspended during wartime. I told him that the sense of belonging was one of the great gifts men get in battle.

He listened, rather sadly, I guess, but he didn't say anything more.

No visits from Anjang while we've been traveling. Maybe tonight? I feel excited about it, like I would when I'd made a heavy date.

10

STILL HAVEN'T PICKED UP MY JOURNAL AGAIN, OR WORKED
on the map. It feels like we're on holiday here. Or maybe like
camp. I used to go to Boy Scout camp at Cleawox just outside of Florence on the coast every summer. Loved it.

Every morning Uda asks me about my dreams. I thought
he was interested because I had the attack dream, but it
seems it's much more than that. I tell him a little about my
visits from Anjang—she did come again last night. I would
like to ask Uda why she rebuffs my attempts to make love to
her. We're already more intimate than I've ever been with
any girl in my whole life. Still haven't figured out a way to
approach the subject.

I've noticed that after any sleeping period the whole
group sits together, usually in a circle around the fire. Each
one, including B'ma, speaks for a while. After one speaks
several of the others may comment, but not always. I had
assumed this was a kind of democratic bull session, strate-
gizing the plans for the day. Turns out it's a dream round
robin! I was included for the first time this morning. Uda
asked me if I had good dreams, and I talked a little about my
visit from Anjang, leaving out the most important details, of
course. Uda translated for the others. Then I thought the
strategy session would take place, but instead B'ma started
telling his dream. Uda was translating it for me at first, but

as B'ma continued, great big tears began rolling down his face. Pretty soon everyone was crying. I had a devil of a time finding out why.

During our absence—how funny that I thought of it as "our" absence, even though I've haven't even been there yet! Anyway, a child has died, or "gone home," as Uda put it. It may be Sua's daughter, or Ete's daughter, or B'ma's sister. The terms "daughter" and "sister" seem to refer to something other than blood relationships. Anyway, everyone cried for quite a while after B'ma told his dream, grabbing handfuls of ashes from the fire and spreading them over their hair and bodies.

Next we did some sad singing. One person would sing a solo while the rest provided a chorus and musical accompaniment made by clicking small rocks together. When it was my turn I performed a touching rendition of "Home on the Range," which was very well received. After the first verse the rest of the group joined in on the chorus—"Home, home on the range, where the deer and the antelope play"—which sounded more like, "Oma, oma, rangey, deerantel oplay."

We were all quiet and sad for a while, just sitting around the fire, humming a little. Then at some cue that I must have missed, Masamo and Heeta rose, briskly washed themselves in the pool until all trace of ash was removed, gathered their weapons, and left camp. Uda says they must provide supplies for tonight's feast. Apparently we first mourn the loss of the departed and then celebrate her homecoming. He asks me again if "the others" have visited me, but when I say "No," and "What others are you talking about?" he ignores the question.

I also asked about B'ma's dream. Shouldn't we have confirmed the child's death before we celebrated it, I wanted to know? Uda is brisk now. He and B'ma have brought out a quantity of some kind of thick vine that B'ma gathered yesterday while the others hunted. It has been soaking in water and they have spread it over a fallen tree trunk and are pounding it with the edge of a stone. I manage to drag myself over to them by sliding and pulling my mat across the ground with my good arm. I must get Masamo to cut me a strong, forked branch for a crutch. I think I could get around with one now.

When I got Uda to stop his industrious pounding for a while, I managed to extract some information of considerable interest. B'ma is something they call a "waking dreamer," as is Anjang. B'ma has come with them on this dangerous journey like a kind of walkie-talkie. He apparently stays in contact with the rest of the tribe in his nightly dreams!

I don't know why this is so startling to me; after all, I've been meeting with Anjang regularly. I guess I think of our meetings as mostly a sexual thing. Uda says this ability—not the sexual thing, but "waking dreaming"—is quite common, but that B'ma and Anjang have developed it to a high degree, or maybe it's a gift. I'm not sure of the distinction. I asked Uda if dreams were always true. Without any hesitation he said, "Yes." A moment later he added that although dreams were always true, men did not always understand them at first. He added that any important dream would come back again and again until you got the message.

B'ma helped organize me so I can join the pounding of the vine. I'm braced against one log with another next to my good arm so I can whack away with it. I had the idea he and Uda were working on some part of our feast for tonight, an idea that amused them no end. Turns out we're making clothes!

I want to have some more discussion about the "waking dream" thing. For example, could I meet Anjang if I didn't drink the green cocktail? Do I have the gift? Or is it something Anjang can do with everyone? For once Uda doesn't seem very interested in the subject of dreaming. He and B'ma are engaged in intense conversation. When I finally get Uda to translate some of it for me, it turns out they're discussing the decoration of the clothing we're making and what kinds of plants for dyeing can be found near the camp. Uda rather sternly suggests that I stop bothering him and think about what designs I want to use. If I draw them in the dirt then B'ma will help me. So here I am, deep in the jungle, on the run from savages armed with Arisakas—whom I apparently must avoid killing—and I'm planning the designs I'm going to use on a new wardrobe! B'ma asks me if I prefer blue or brown. At least I think that's what he is asking. He points to various patterns on my jungle jock and says something that sounds like a question. And now, like a real doofus, I'm starting to think about it. Red is what I want, of course. I want to decorate my thing, my wrap, I guess, with a Stewart hunting plaid.

The Christmas I was five years old my Grandmother Stewart gave me a kilt for a present. To say I was pleased is something of an understatement. I loved it so much I insisted on sleeping in it for the first night. I wore it to kindergarten and punched anyone who laughed at me and said only girls wore skirts. Grandma Stewart kept me well supplied with kilts of the appropriate size until I was an adult. I wore a kilt with a white dinner jacket to my senior prom; I wore one under my robe for graduation. Other kids used to specify when I was invited to events that kilts were not acceptable attire. I usually wore one anyway. You can see where the "Kilty" came from.

Maybe I could do a Royal Stewart plaid? Use blue and brown instead of blue and green. I am trying to get the lines right, drawing in the dirt with a sharp stick. Hard to achieve a satisfactory effect. I might have to settle for a tic-tac-toe design with "Kilroy Was Here" as a border. I was never very good with art.

⚮ 11 ⚭

I WOKE UP AT DAWN PRETTY HUNGOVER FROM FERMENTED honey. From the looks of the camp I'm not the only one. I seem to have missed most of the party. The singing and dancing were just getting underway when I crawled into the lean-to and passed out. At least I can manage to move about on my own, using the crutch made from a forked stick Masamo cut yesterday for me. I've had a terrible dream. I don't want to discuss it with anyone. It's not an attack dream or anything like that, nothing that has to do with the group or our safety. It's personal.

Eventually everyone rouses. I've arranged myself by the pool with my mat, journal, and pencils. Finally I'm working on a map. No one is very lively. Hecta gets up and starts making some breakfast—a mash of tubers that have been cooked in the ashes with acornlike nuts and some berries. My intention is to wave breakfast off, but turns out I'm too hungry to say no to food. I hope there's no dream circle this morning—everyone is hung. But I'm wrong. As soon as the food is gone we all gather around the fire.

The twins report first. They usually dream about game and hunting. B'ma gives a longish report on events at home, a morning news show. Uda only translates a few words for me now and then. When my turn comes I shine everyone on, saying something about the usual visit from Anjang. Uda almost questions me about it, but lets it go. He's too sharp to miss my uneasiness, but he doesn't say anything. Then it's Masamo's turn. He's troubled too.

He tells a dream that goes something like this. We are crossing some sort of vine bridge over a chasm. I am being carried in the hammock like before. "The fools" are behind us, trying to cut the lines that support the bridge—or untying them. Anyway, the bridge starts to go. Here Masamo becomes very excited and everyone has something to say about it. Takes a while for Uda to catch me up. The upshot is that everyone makes it off the bridge to the other side except for Masamo and me. We're just hanging there when the bridge falls free, or swings free from the one side. I'm not sure about that part. So we're hanging there together. Now "the fools" are shooting at us with bows and arrows. Uda asks Masamo why he doesn't let go. Masamo says that he is afraid that I don't know how to fly and that I will be frightened and fall if he doesn't stay with me.

Everyone nods agreement at this. Everybody seems worried now, and there is a lot of rapid speech with emphatic gestures. The twins get up to leave. They both dreamed about some animal, a kind of a small deer, and they have to leave now if they're going to get to the place where they saw it in time to capture it or kill it. Heeta stands up and tells them they can't leave yet. All three of them are yelling at one another. I have a really terrible headache by now. Uda isn't paying much attention to the yelling match, but he's watching me carefully. I ignore him.

B'ma goes to stand between the twins and Heeta, spreading his arms out to make some distance between them. He doesn't say anything, just holds them apart. They stop yelling, and all three leave together. B'ma tags after them. Masamo is still worried, I guess. He keeps looking at me apologetically, like he let me down in some way. I really don't want to talk about it. I grab my crutch and hobble to the pool where I left my notebook and pencils. I go back to designing my map, ignoring Uda and Masamo. The two of them dig out the vines we were working on yesterday. They've been buried in some mud. Now they've turned a grayish blue color. Uda and Masamo sit down together and pound them some more—without talking. The vines are beginning to flatten out, like long sheets of thick, bluish paper.

I'm more realistic today. As I look around at the camp that seemed so idyllic, I begin to notice things I missed before. Everything looks dirty. Gnats and flies are buzzing around spots where honey was spilled and food has been dropped. Some have found me out and keep bothering me as I labor over my rough map. I begin to realize I've been kidding myself. Just what do I think I'm doing, anyway? I should be making plans. It won't be long before I can travel on my own. I need to learn more about the surrounding tribes—maybe I can get some help from them when I leave. I need to learn which vines produce those edible tubers and how to recognize which berries are good. I need to ask Uda which direction he traveled when he went to the clinic.

While I am descending into this pit of dissatisfaction B'ma comes back. He walks towards me carrying a bunch of leaf bundles that he has tied with a long vine and slung over his shoulder. His face is completely untroubled, and he gives me a smile of such total trust—and grace, I guess that's the word. My feeling of uneasiness doesn't disappear, but I can't respond to his open nature with anything less than real affection.

"Holy cow, Keeltee!" he says by way of greeting. "Holy cow, B'ma," I respond with as much warmth as I can summon. Then he starts pointing at his bundles, obviously delighted with himself. We somehow carry on a conversation. I say, "What have you got there, B'ma?" He laughs, joyously, and shakes his head, saying something in S'norran that I take to be "I bet you can't guess?" To which I reply, "Peanut butter cookies and Tootsie Rolls, I bet." And maybe he says, "Not quite, but close." Neither of us could follow the words, natch, but the inflection was familiar—and the game must be one played by kids and their pals all over the world.

After we've gone on this way for a while B'ma gestures for me to close my eyes and stick out my arm. I am relieved that it is my arm he wants me to stick out, to tell the truth. Once before when he had me close my eyes and open my mouth, I was rewarded with some alarming S'norran delicacy that I felt honor bound to chew up and swallow. Whatever it was stayed alive and kicking all the way down to my stomach.

I close my eyes and stick out my arm. Then I feel him stroking it with a finger, smearing something over a good-sized area. "Okay," he says, or some S'norran word to that effect.

I open my eyes and look to see. "Holy cow!" I am genuinely amazed. B'ma has painted my arm red with something he is carrying in one of his bundles. Not exactly red, more like the color of iron rust, but hey, we're in the jungle. The day before I had showed him the worn-down eraser on one of my pencils to indicate what color I needed. He's a pretty amazing kid to go out and find something so damn close to it! He's watching my face carefully and, finally says, "Good,

54

Keeltee?" in English, no less. Now I'm really knocked out. Touched, I guess you'd say.

In the meantime Uda and Masamo have stopped pounding on the bark cloth and have drifted over our way. We're all sitting down together in a loose circle next to the pool, and I can tell something's up. I may be charmed by B'ma's sincerity, but that doesn't mean I'm going to spill my guts to them.

B'ma opens his other bundles and shows us some black and brown stuff. Uda and Masamo are pleased, but it's pretty clear that's not why they came over, to look at the dyes. Uda announces that Masamo wants to tell me a story. So I agree to listen to him. I've been very well treated by these people. They saved my life and they're good people. They deserve some courtesy from me, even if I don't necessarily want to share their rituals. I'm not a shy kind of guy, but I'm just not used to talking about the most intimate details of my life, or of my dreams, with other folks. That doesn't mean I don't think it's fine for them to do it. After all, it's their country and I'm just a visitor here, even though I'm feeling like a pretty reluctant visitor today.

So everybody settles down for story time. B'ma leaves for a minute and comes back with a wide leaf with a long stem, which he uses as a whisk to keep insects away. Masamo clears his throat and then starts talking in a singsong voice. He speaks for a short time and then stops so that Uda can explain his words to me. What he says is something like this:

Many years ago when I am little I am dreaming every night that I fall. Sometimes I am falling from tops of high trees. Other times from walls, or from mountainsides. I am swinging from vines and falling. I am climbing for fruits and falling. I am climbing for honey and falling. Every day I am telling my fathers and mothers of my falling. I am falling and falling and falling.

So my mothers and fathers are saying to me: This is very good dream, Masamo. You are brave boy to have so many good falling dreams. Then they ask me, *"What happens when you are falling?"* Every day mothers and fathers ask me, *"What happens when you are falling?"* And I answer, *"I am waking, of course. I am very frightened when I am falling, and I am waking."*

When this part has been recited and translated we take a little break while Uda and Masamo discuss something. Then Masamo continues:

My mothers and fathers say to me, "Falling in dreams is very good, Masamo, and you are only a little boy to have such a big dream so early and so many times. Now you are ready to learn a very big secret, and you are little to learn this secret so soon."

They tell me that I must not wake up when I am falling, I must fall and fall, and when I can do this, then I will be somewhere else!

Another pause for translation. Everyone nods when Uda gets to the "somewhere else" part. B'ma interrupts, and then Uda adds that B'ma wishes me to know that he also had the falling dream when he was very little.

Masamo continues.

So I am trying. For many nights I am trying. And when I am awake I am trying. I am telling myself the story of my dream, and when I begin to fall I do not wake up in the story I tell myself—I just fall and fall, but I do not land yet.

And then one night when I am sleeping I am dreaming that I am picking some fruits from a high tree near the cliff. I am leaning way out to get a very good fruit and I slip and start to fall. But I catch a branch, and for a moment I am good— then the branch breaks, and I fall again! I am going to fall over the cliff, and I am very much afraid now. But there is a bush growing at the edge. I grab the bush and stop my fall. But the bush is not strong, and it begins to pull away from the ground and now the bush and I are falling over the edge of the cliff.

Another pause for translation here. Masamo is a good storyteller. We're all into it now.

But this time I do not wake up. I am falling and falling for a very longtime. And I land somewhere else. I am in a place of many beautiful lights. I am feeling so happy to be there. I am looking, looking, and the lights are so beautiful and the air is so good. I am smelling wonderful smells I have never smelled before. And then it happens. . . .

He pauses. Uda translates. This guy should write Saturday morning serials, I'm thinking.

The spirits come to me. And they say, "Masamo, you are a very brave boy. You are ready to fly." And the spirits teach me to fly. Now I am never falling again. I am a dream flyer.

After Uda translates this part we are all silent for a while. I am remembering the day I soloed for the first time—no instructor sitting behind me in that noisy little, rattling, yellow Aronca. I thought my life was going to be perfect from that moment on. Masamo and B'ma rise and go to the edge of the pool, slipping into the water very quietly. Uda stays with me.

"You are dream flyer, Keeltee?" he asks.

I have to think about the question. It seems to have many different kinds of meaning. I ponder. The night after my first solo flight I dreamed I was flying. "Sometimes," I answer.

Now he is thoughtful. "Flying dreams very good, Keel-tee. But bad dreams good, too." He watches me, waiting.

I'm not going to fall for this one. "Yeah," I say in a flat voice.

Uda is quiet. When I don't continue, he begins to talk to me about Masamo's dream from the night before. He says it is likely that Masamo will be called upon to do something for me, something that requires great courage or strength. He says this doesn't necessarily mean Masamo will save my life; it could be a different sort of courage. He adds in a casual way that as long as we stay in the good place we are safe from "the animals" and "the fools," but it is likely "the fools" will be around when we reach the crossing. He says a crossing is always an important event, watching me closely as he speaks.

I am beginning to feel worried again. As my strength returns the idea of being carried helpless in a hammock while all kinds of things endanger us is more than a bit unnerving.

~~ 12 ~~

I WAKE UP FROM THE TERRIBLE DREAM, MY BODY COVERED with greasy sweat, my heart pounding. I grope around until I find my crutch and then crawl out of the lean-to. The others are sleeping in a separate structure a few yards away. If I'm careful I can slip pass them and get to the pool, where I'll be able to rinse off and refresh myself. Maybe I'll just stay up. Anything to avoid that dream. I sure don't want to sleep again if it means having that dream return.

As I might have expected, Uda is sitting by the small fire between the lean-tos. I know he has been waiting for me.

"Sit, Keeltee." His voice is firm. It is not exactly an order, but he speaks with quiet authority. I ease myself down onto the end of a log that has been placed there for my convenience. The others usually sit on large, thick leaves, arranging them carefully underneath themselves. They don't like to sit on dirt.

"Drink this." Uda hands me a half gourd into which he has ladled something from a pot sitting at the edge of the fire. It smells like the fragrance that I associate with him. I take a sip of the tea, savoring its taste, smoky, sweet, and yet salty at the same time.

"Good," I mumble.

"Tea for good dreams, Keeltee." He pulls a piece of wood from the fire and waves it in front of my face. The smoke smells sweet and tangy like the tea.

"Leaves make tea. Wood makes good smoke."

The sweat is drying now. My skin feels cooler while I am warmed inside from the tangy brew. Above us a myriad of stars fills the sky. I am looking up, trying to locate familiar patterns when Uda picks up a stick and points at a cluster to the east of the handle of the Big Dipper, which hangs low in the west.

"S'norr," he says.

I frown, uncomprehending. In the flickering light of the fire he draws a design in the dirt. First the Big Dipper. He speaks a word in S'norran, pointing at the ground, then to the sky.

"Big Dipper," I respond.

Following the handle of the Dipper he now creates an additional pattern of six stars, one of which I think I recognize as Arcturus. He points at the sky and says a different word, then to the ground.

"Arcturus," I say, since I don't know the name of this constellation.

Uda circles one of the points above and to the right of the star I think is Arcturus, saying firmly, "S'norr." Next he points up at the sky and says, "S'norr," then back at the pattern on the ground, "S'norr."

I don't know the name of the star he points at. I'm not sure I want to pursue the matter. He waits for a moment. Then points again, first to the circle on the ground, then up to the sky, each time speaking in that calm, authoritative voice. "S'norr."

I look at him though the tendrils of sweet smoke spiraling up from the small fire. "You're telling me that S'norr is a star, Uda? That you come from a star called S'norr?"

Uda is smiling now, with his full turtleness look. The fire illuminates the network of fine wrinkles in his golden skin, which I find, for some reason, deeply endearing. He begins rocking, ever so slightly, back and forth. He tells me this story.

Long, long, longtime ago, Keeltee, before people were. Before animals were. Before plants were. We come. We come in dreams. We come to wind. We come to air. We come to water and to rain. We come to fire. We see it is good here. We come to watch and to wait.

He smiles and stirs the fire so that the sweet smoke rises around us. Then he continues.

Long, longtime ago, before people were. Before animals were. We come. We come in dreams. We come to grass. We come to trees. We come to vines. We come to good roots in ground. We come to leaves. Then sometime we come to flowers. We gather in flowers. We gather in fruits. We watch and we wait. We see it is good here.

He rocks a little, breathing the smoke.

Long, long, longtime we come. Before people were. We come. We come in tigers. We come in spiders and in monkeys. We come in beetles. We come in honey birds and serpents. We come in bees. We come in deer and in fishes. Oh, and it is good here. We see it is good. We watch and we wait.

Now sometime people were. Long, longtime we watch people. We watch in dreams of people. We gather in dreams of people. We show people it is good. Earth is good. Water is good. We show people good plants. We show in dreams. We show people good animals. We show in dreams.

Then longtime we come in people. One, two, not many. We gather in people until we are few, not many. We come here and there. We come in people of many lands. We come to people of cold lands. We come in dreams. We come to people of dry lands. We come in dreams.

Uda stands now and begins to act out the story. He shows me people of the kangaroo, people of the polar bear, people of the reindeer, people of the buffalo and of the elephant. He acts out these animals until I recognize and identify them. When I understand he goes on.

Now, Keeltee. Most important. We have come in people of jumping-around animal, in people of large white growling animal, in people of animals with trees on head, in people of thundering feet animal and people of long nose animal. This is good. But all these who have come forget the secrets. Some maybe keep one little piece of secret. Others keep maybe two or three little pieces of secret. Secret of dreaming is lost to people of this place. Secret of returning home, home to S'norr, is lost. All lost to people of this place.

He is quiet for a while. Together we breathe the smoke. He speaks again.

Only here do we remember. Only here. We watch and we wait. We remember all secrets. We remember how to dream. We remember returning home to S'norr secret. We wait for messenger. When messenger comes all return home. All return home to S'norr.

We sit together for a while gazing into the firelight, and then I go back to bed. My terrible dream doesn't return.

❧ 13 ❧

October 25, 1944

I grew up in a place where you court the sun—always crossing over to walk on the sunny side of the street, moving your chair to the window to catch the early morning rays—the threat of rain is always present in Oregon, even in the midst of the hottest summer. Now here I am, seeking out the shadiest spot to perch. Struck me this morning how unusual that is. I know there is a monsoon season here. Fortunately for me it won't start again until February or March. There is no doubt in my mind that by then I will have found some way to get back to my outfit.

Uda has suggested that I write my bad dream down in my journal. In the morning bull session I did say I had the bad dream again, but that I didn't want to talk about it. I guess I don't really want to write about it either. I keep thinking of other things to write here.

Well, here goes. I am back in the Dan Moore Hotel in Portland. It's the night before the championship game with Beaverton and Binky Druitt has found a couple of sluts in some roadhouse. The team is taking turns with them. That's the way the dream usually goes. I guess I've been having it recur for a long time. Last night and the night before it was pretty much the same—except for one major difference. Just thinking about it or writing it down makes me sick, like I want to vomit. Here goes nothing.

I'm standing in line, waiting my turn. Now I can see the girl. It's not the slut; it's Anjang. Her apricot skin is slimy with sweat and bodily fluids. I can smell it. Lined up in front of me are my crew from *Paper Doll*. Rusty is just climbing on top of her.

I had to stop writing there and go down to the pool for a while to cool off in the water. I can get in and out by myself now. I am going to finish this now. Then I'll go and work on my piece of bark cloth. I learned yesterday that we're making presents to take back to the rest of the tribe! Can you beat that? Turns out that this is the only mud that makes the gray-blue color on the cloth. There's something kind of funny about it. I seem to be allied with a tribe that is facing extinction. I may be facing likely death myself. I try not to think about that. And here we are, delaying our journey back to safety to color some strips of cloth with special mud because they'll make good presents. There must be something more to this. I tried to question Uda about the logic of it, but I get the usual: "Because we are the people of the dream." I asked if the color has a special religious importance. It was pretty tough getting that concept across. Finally Uda explained to me that the women feel the blue color looks especially well in the sunlight.

I guess it's obvious that I don't want to write about my dream.

Anyway, when Rusty climbs on top of Anjang she turns her head towards me and the same look is on her face as I saw on the slut. It's that look of pain and loathing. In the dream I leap out of line. I want to pull her away, to rescue her from such humiliation. I yell, "Anjang!" But the other guys grab me and tell me I have to wait my turn. That's when I wake up.

There, I've done it. Can't say I feel much better about any-thing. I'm going to join Uda and B'ma now. Finish the design on my bark cloth.

I'm working hard on my Royal Stewart, painting squares of red that allow blue lines to show through. We're all three pretty intent on our work. Uda asks me if writing my dream down made me feel better. I answer, "Not really." B'ma is helping me get my lines straight. It's pretty amazing. Both he and Uda take my artistry quite seriously. B'ma asks me a question, which Uda translates.

"B'ma asks how you felt in your dream?" B'ma looks at me with a smile of such unaffected sweetness. There is real concern on his face—reminds me of when he was taking care of me in the first hut when I was in so much pain. I think about the question for a while. Then I tell Uda that I felt embarrassment, anger, and confusion, not necessarily in that order. Uda nods thoughtfully and explains to B'ma, who also nods and smiles encouragement at me. Part of me wants to tell them to lay off. I really don't want to talk about it. But now there's another feeling, almost like I want to get something off my chest. It's like the nausea I felt a short time ago. If I could just rid myself of something I know I'd feel so much better.

Uda says, "Keeltee, you have these feelings now?"

"You mean at this moment?"

"At this moment."

"No. Not now."

"When?" Again he speaks with a voice of such simple, compelling authority.

Without thinking I answer, "When I am with Anjang in my dreams, we are very, very close." I look to see if he under-stands what I mean, but his face is quite neutral.

"Close, yes. Anjang very good healer."

"No. It's more than that. She—she does things, intimate things—but . . ." I just can't explain it. I look at Uda, who waits, his face serene. B'ma is concentrating on his piece of bark cloth.

I gesture helplessly. "She doesn't let *me* make love to *her!*" It's out.

Uda nods and says, "Anjang will not laugh with you."

"What?"

Now to my genuine concern he translates for B'ma, who frowns and nods sympathetically at me. What's wrong with these people? This kid can't be more than ten years old. I wouldn't have said anything if I'd known Uda would translate.

It gets worse. Uda now makes the classic hand gesture for jerking someone off and then another for blow job. He says, "This and this, yes?" Then he makes the gesture for intercourse, index finger of left hand plunging in and out of a circle formed by thumb and forefinger of the other hand, and he says, "Not this."

I can't believe it. I can't believe someone of such dignity and authority would be so vulgar. I'm embarrassed for Uda. I'm really upset about B'ma hearing and seeing this. Sputtering to myself in indignation, I manage to struggle to my feet and hobble away from them both.

But now Uda is relentless. He follows me and sits down on the ground without even bothering to find a leaf to put beneath him. He just drops by my feet and looks up at me.

"Why angry, Keeltee?"

I have to explain that in my country we don't use those gestures in relation to women that we care about, and we certainly don't discuss such matters or make these gestures in front of children. It is easier than I expected to explain. Uda observes that the English at the clinic also had much shame about these matters. He adds gravely that he understands now that I wish "to laugh" with Anjang. He says that this may be possible, but first all parties must agree and a ceremony will be required.

It seems odd, but I feel greatly relieved by his words. I assume that I must be accepted by the tribe in some formal way, some kind of initiation or something. I seem to remember that American Indians would sometimes accept whites after a ceremony that involved smoking some tobacco together. I think I can handle that. By now I'll agree to almost anything if it means I can look forward to sleeping with Anjang, really sleeping with her, I mean, not to mention being free from that gross, disturbing dream.

So I tell Uda I'd like to have that ceremony. He nods and says simply, "First, all must agree."

I'm about to get up and go back to my bark cloth, but Uda stops me.

"Others are in dream, Keeltee?"

I frown, confused. "What others?"

"B'ma says others cannot get home. Men you are flying with caught in bad place. Bad dream place."

"Oh shit." There's just no escaping it. I give up and tell Uda the entire dream, going all the way back to my experience in high school. It's not an easy job, you can believe, although the hardest thing, oddly enough, is explaining the significance of the state basketball tournament. I finally remember that Uda lived with the British and I ask him if they played cricket. At that a look of complete comprehension comes over his face and he laughs at some length. Now I have to agree that cricket is a foolish sport, but try as I might I can't explain to him why basketball is much different.

Uda tells me that my men are caught in a kind of hell place, as indicated by their appearance in my nightmare. He says this is not unusual when men have died violently and unexpectedly in battle, although he seems surprised that they couldn't fly on home given that they died in a plane. This speculation is quite beyond me. He asks me if they have had some bad dreams before their death time. Christ! How would I know? I tell him we don't make a practice of telling our dreams over breakfast. I can tell he is not that surprised, but he is still troubled. He asks me how we prepare for our death in battle if we don't tell one another our dreams? I reply that we don't prepare for our death in battle. For a moment a look of pure horror passes over Uda's face. His eyes darken, and color drains from his golden skin. I am shocked by his change of expression and make a gesture towards him. He quickly stands and moves away, his back to me. A moment later he returns, his face composed.

"Men in very bad place, Keeltee. Not good. We must help them come home."

14

I MAY BE LIVING IN A DREAM WORLD. THE WAR SEEMS SO FAR away, real life so distant. This morning's bull session was extraordinary. I don't quite know how it happened, but everyone seemed to know about my dream, with all its lurid details. The sexual part, which for me is where the horror lies, isn't of much concern to the others. They are disturbed, alarmed even, by the fact that my men have not "gone home." Apparently there was some hope that they would appear to one of the others. Then my men would have their help, I assume. No one seems to look at my nightmare as an illusion. I asked Uda what dreams were. He said that dreams are real; they are events that happen while we sleep. In other words, my men appeared in my nightmare the way a visitor shows up at your house in the evening. Uda and the others believe my men are "angry, confused, and embarrassed." A long discussion took place around why they might have these feelings. There was indeed a general feeling of dismay when Uda explained to the others that my men had no preparation for death in battle.

To tell the truth, I just don't quite get it. It seems we can't make the crossing until I help my men "go home." So here we are. Sua and Heeta have gone on a reconnaissance mission to the place of crossing, apparently to ascertain whether or not "the fools" are waiting for us there. Uda believes we

are safe from attack as long as we stay in this "good place."
I ask why that is. He tells me that "the animals" and "the
fools" are very superstitious people, afraid of the ghost beast
and other beasts that belong to the S'norra. In the past when
either group was so foolish as to venture here, they would
be attacked by these beasts and flee in terror. I ask if we can
send the beasts to frighten them now, but Uda tells me we
don't have the beasts with us; they have been left with the
rest of the tribe on the other side of the crossing.

I should probably have let it drop here, but I really want
to understand, so I ask Uda to tell me more about the beasts.
He is thoughtful and quiet, then nods to himself. He explains
that the ghost beast is a very powerful weapon, which was
given to one of Heeta's ancestors by the spirits in a great
dream. It has protected the S'norra for many generations.
The two other beasts, the thunder beast and the lightning
beast, were given to Uda when he worked at the clinic, also
in a great dream. He brought them back with him. He says
they are quite effective with "the animals" and "the fools,"
but he is not certain they would frighten the Japanese. He
tells me that the Japanese have many terrifying beasts of their
own, and that the threatening tribes are bolder than ever
before with their protection.

Now Uda explains to me that a long, longtime ago, the
ancestors learned in a dream that men who have been exposed
to the violence of battle must be healed before they can return to
the tribe. He used the word "wounded," and I thought he was
speaking of wounds to the body, but it seems he is including
other kinds of wounds, what we call shell shock or battle
fatigue. As far as I can tell, the S'norra believe that any violence produces bad dreams.

When I ask Uda how these men are healed after battle, he is surprised by my question. He explains that Anjang has been healing me for some days now and apparently has the intention of helping my men.

I get pretty upset at this, you can bet. The last thing I want is for Anjang to be massaging and fondling the others the way she does me almost every night. I forget for the moment that the men I am jealous of are already dead.

We are lazing by the pool, watching the rippling patterns that the light breeze makes moving across the water. There is a group of salamanders hunting around the submerged stump of some ancient tree a few feet beneath the surface of the pool. One will float to the surface, gulp a breath of air and then work its way back down, flashing a beautifully mottled orange and yellow underbelly as it does.

I am essentially a practical man, and practically speaking, if we cannot cross until my men are home, I guess I had better find out how to help them get there. I have avoided asking Uda just what constitutes a "crossing," although the memory of Masamo's dream of a vine bridge, especially the image of me strapped in my carrier, dangling from the end of it, scares the life out of me.

"So, Uda, just how can I help my men get home?"

At this question, Uda turns to me with a look of such joyful satisfaction that I feel like I've won the lottery.

"Ah yes, Keeltee. I have been asking this myself. Too late to prepare these men for death in battle, men totally dead forever. These good men, yes?"

"The best."

"So, Keeltee, one question. In bad dream Anjang is laughing with these men, yes?"

71

By now I've figured out that "laughing with someone" to the S'norra means sexual intercourse. So I nod perfunctorily.

"Anjang in dream angry, tearful, yes? Not happy with men? Slut in old dream not happy with you? Not laughing?"

"There is no laughing, Uda—it's a bloody nightmare for heaven's sake!"

"I am thinking, Keeltee, maybe men cannot get home yet. I have one idea. I must go walk, walk a little. Talk to trees about it. You look in water here. Ask water about a good place where men can go. Place where men can be with Anjang, some other good sluts, too, maybe. I walk short time. Come back."

15

October 27, 1944

Dear Diary,

Funny how I want to start today's entry with those words. I kept a diary for only three months one summer. I was given a blue leather one with a strap and a small key, for my fourteenth birthday, I guess. I really did write all my dreams down in it.

Well, I did it! Last night I took all the guys to the USO. It was really something. Uda and I worked all yesterday afternoon getting the details just right. I remembered a great place, just off Market Street in San Francisco. I actually went there with Rusty before we shipped out. There was a bandstand and lots of great-looking gals to dance with. The usual coffee and doughnuts were served, Coca-Cola, too, I think.

The trickiest part was getting Anjang there, but I finally was able to see her dressed up in a sharp little Dorothy Lamour sarong number. In my dream last night she was behind the bar pouring coffee. I lined the men up in front of her and introduced them one at a time. She shook hands with most of them, but Rusty got a big buss on the cheek, like from a big sister. Tom Tully cried a little. He's a tough little runt, my tail gunner, part Cherokee, rode halfway across the country on the rails to enlist. Told 'em he was eighteen when he was barely sixteen. Anjang looked into my eyes, told me I'd done good—now she and the other sluts could take care of the men!

I guess we're stuck with the word "sluts." Uda asked me what it meant when I was telling him the old state basketball tournament nightmare, and I said sluts were "easy women," which he took to mean something good. Well, who knows—maybe it does.

It was pretty interesting yesterday. Uda had me close my eyes and remember the USO as vividly as possible. I think I did a bang-up job. I could even smell the place—especially when I got near the men's head—and hear Benny Goodman's orchestra on the bandstand (nothing but the best for those guys!), and taste those goddamn sugared doughnuts. I kept thinking of all the varieties—spudnuts, I always loved spudnuts, puffy glazed doughnuts, doughnuts with thick, dark chocolate frosting and chopped walnuts on top. I just can't get enough to eat here. I keep hoping there'll be more food when we reach the others.

So last night when I went to bed, I started running the whole thing in my mind like I was going to a movie. I started with the men. Got 'em all lined up before we went in. Then, quick as a wink, we were there, and I could see Anjang waiting behind the counter with all those damn doughnuts.

It's a funny thing—to imagine a USO club as a halfway house to heaven, but I guess it worked, because when I told my dream this morning and Uda translated everyone nodded and smiled. Some discussion followed. Essentially the question seemed to be whether or not my men were safe. It's agreed they are not home yet, but they are in a good place, or a place of good dreaming. The consensus is that we can head for the crossing. Sua and Heeta returned quite late last night. "The fools" weren't at the crossing place, but they found traces suggesting they had been there recently.

After this I thought we were finished, but Heeta spoke at some length, drawing some lines in the dirt with a stick and pointing at different places when he spoke. There was a moment of silence,

Uda looked at Heeta for a while without speaking. Then a short discussion followed, finally ending with Heeta speaking again, firmly and briefly. Uda said to me that Heeta had received a dream during the night that told how to handle "the fools." He didn't elaborate on the plans.

I'm to have my leg cast completely off before we leave. It's gotten pretty beaten up in any case. Uda says the shoulder cast should stay on to provide support when I'm in the hammock. I'm practically bursting with energy this morning. It's funny, getting those men into the USO last night gave me such a big kick. I think I could take on "the animals" and "the fools" myself single-handed.

This morning Uda produced my boots and socks from somewhere in the bottom of his carrying basket. Can't believe how happy I am to have them on. It's one thing to hop barefooted around the camp where the ground is clear and reasonably flat. I'd be a goner if I had to start racing barefooted through the jungle the way the others do. Boots are a bit singed on the edges, but what the hey! I'm feeling really great today. What an adventure this is! Maybe I'll write a book about it when I get home. Can't help thinking that soon I'll be seeing Anjang in the flesh. Taking her in my arms. I already know what her voice sounds like, how sweetly she smells, the smooth texture of her apricot skin. But to actually hold her!

ᴀ 16 ᴀ

THERE ARE SOME THINGS I LIKE ABOUT BEING CARRIED IN A hammock. The view is one of them. All day we've traveled through country of immense beauty. Sometimes the leafy canopy is far above, the ground beneath open and welcoming with little undergrowth to slow our travel. Then the jungle closes in, with paths so narrow and foliage so low that the others have to crouch as they force their way through the dense barrier. At times we seem to move through a narrow green tunnel that closes behind us as soon as we pass. I had expected we would travel as silently as possible—the ability of my companions to move through even the densest growth without a sound is astonishing—however, there is constant loud chatter, much laughter, and even singing. At one of our frequent rest breaks Uda explained that it was necessary to make enough noise to scare any animals (the real ones, not the natives) that might attack us if we came upon them unaware.

In the early afternoon we passed through a glade filled with large boulders covered with thick green moss. It reminded me of a place up the McKenzie Pass, on the trail to Proxy Falls, where great, rough boulders of ancient lava have grown moss overcoats so dense that they appear to be soft and cushiony. The smell here is so intense, full and rich and often perfumy, although I haven't seen any flowers—nothing is red or yellow, just varying shades of green. It is so green under the trees that it feels almost like being underwater.

I am awake, but I feel dreamy, swaying along, gazing up at the complex patterns of light and shadow so far above. Oddly enough, my dreams are becoming more real. The other night, when I successfully got my men to the USO club, it was as solid and physical to me as any real life experience. When I am with Anjang it feels like I am really with her, even though I usually can remember that we're in a dream together. I don't understand this at all.

We are short one man today. Most of the time I am being carried by two of the men, while the third walks alongside. At each rest stop there's a switch. When the going is rougher, the third person takes a hand and sometimes Uda also. Before we got to the good place, my hammock was slung between two long poles, two men at each end. Now there's just one pole with a single man at either end. My crutch is lashed to the pole. We still move as rapidly as I could have traveled on foot.

Heeta left early in the morning with two of the detonators. He will probably join us tonight, after locating "the fools." If he doesn't appear we're to wait on him at an agreed-on spot not too far from the crossing place. I believe the plan is for him to use the detonators to frighten "the fools" so that they run away and we can safely cross. His carrying basket was left at the good place, tied up in a tree to be safe from animals and disguised with leaves. When he left, in addition to the detonators, he carried his blowgun and almost all the arrows, those belonging to the others as well as his own.

Turns out that Heeta is the father of Sua and Ete. He can't be that much younger than my own dad, although I find that hard to imagine. He's an amazing specimen of a fellow. I have had occasion to touch his arm or lean on his shoulder while I'm getting around. It's like nothing so much as leaning against the trunk of a tree. Completely solid. But he's also as agile as a kid.

My dad will be fifty-six this year. I know he's in pretty good shape for a man of his age, nothing wrong except for a little arthritis, but he seems worn out. Of course, there was the Depression—that took its toll on everyone, even though it wasn't all that hard for us. My dad still had his job as a county surveyor, and Mom was teaching school. We moved out to the ranch and lived with Grandma and Grandpa all one winter, mostly so my mom's brother's family could stay in our house. They lost their own place when they couldn't keep up with the mortgage payments.

Most of the time when I was a kid my folks got up before daylight. My dad drove out to the ranch to help Grandpa with the milking, then came back to town and went to his own job. My folks were happy. They didn't fight or argue, like some others. But I always had a feeling that just getting along was hard work. There wasn't a lot of complaint about it. It's more like a way to measure your worth, if you know what I mean. A good person is someone who works hard without complaining. The harder you work, the less you complain, the better you are.

We were happy and we loved one another. I always felt that I belonged to a loving family—but there wasn't much joyousness in the daily business of life, except for one summer when I worked for Grandpa out at the ranch. I think it was when I turned fourteen. I woke up every morning filled with so much joy that it seemed like I would burst. I couldn't wait for the day to begin, everything seemed so glorious. I developed a habit of putting on clean socks and underpants at night before I went to bed, just so I could get up and out into the new day even faster.

I've been thinking about that summer, swaying along here, looking up at these magnificent trees. I guess it's because I'm feeling that way now. I can hardly wait for each day. Of course I am imagining being with Anjang, that's probably part of it, but I think it's something else as well. It has to do with the S'norra. They are joyous people. When I glance through the mesh of my hammock and catch Masamo's eye, he returns a look that is suffused with joy. God knows he's working hard just now. I'm one hell of a package to carry through this terrain. I guess it's pretty clear that we're all in serious danger from the other tribe, even if no one seems terribly worried about it. But we're still joyful together. Periodically as we travel B'ma will dash off into the surrounding forest and return a few moments later clutching some tubers or wild fruits to share around. There is constant laughter and joking, and it's not like the kind of gallows humor we all fell into during those tense waits between flying sorties—when we made jokes and kidded around to take the edge off the fear. This is something else.

The S'norra seem to feel that life is good. My family—hell, almost everybody in Oregon, not to mention the whole U.S.A.—seems to feel that something out there is going to get you if you don't work hard every minute and keep your defenses up. I'm not a philosopher by any means, and I did read Rousseau in my college philosophy course my last semester at the U. of O. It was right before I joined up. So I know that civilized man likes to fantasize about noble savages and all that business, but these people really are different from anyone I've ever been around. It's true that I haven't been around that much. I do mean to keep my eyes and ears open. But something feels different, so completely different to me. Everybody feels good, free of care. I feel good being with them. Can it be that simple?

☙ 17 ❧

DEEP SILENCE, DISTURBED ONLY WHEN A TROOP OF SCARLET
and blue parrots flies through the treetops overhead uttering
their rough cries. It's been twenty minutes since the first
explosion, and the tension is palpable. I'm stuck in my hammock—they may have to grab me at a moment's notice and
make a run for it—but at least I'm braced against a tree trunk
at an angle so I can see out to the open space in front of us.
Something is wrong. I can feel it. The second explosion ought
to have gone off ten minutes ago. Uda sits with his eyes
closed, but even he is sweating. We are hidden behind a thick
screen of dense growth. I can see to the crossing by parting
the leaves of a massive plant that looks a lot like a split leaf
philodendron, although how we will actually cross is still a
mystery.

The clear space in front of us is flat, about twenty-five to
thirty feet wide. Must be rock with thin soil on top as there
is only sparse grass and moss covering the ground. I can't tell
from here how deep the chasm is, but no treetops show.
It's about ninety feet wide, although a finger of rock juts out
about twelve feet further just in front of us. B'ma is perched
high in the tree above me, Masamo halfway between him
and the ground. We're all pretty tense. The plan, as I understand it, was for Heeta to set off one of the detonators on
the main trail between here and the place where he found

"the fools" camped. It was to be close enough to frighten them, but not so near as to harm anyone. Then he would race to the less frequented trail and set off the second detonator, thus discouraging them from heading in our direction by either route.

At the sound of the second explosion, we were to start the crossing. Heeta would join us, although there is some detail here I didn't quite get when the plan was discussed last night. Heeta didn't stay with us at the temporary camp. He joined us late. Much of the planning was translated for me, but I couldn't follow all the details. Wasn't much time as he had to get back to be in place by morning.

A huge, hairy-legged spider is heading my way again. It is metallic gray, the size of a saucer, only a moment ago seemed poised to jump on the end of the bamboo pole extending out the top of my hammock. It will rest, perfectly still, then move so quickly that I can't follow it with my eyes. I have a horror of it landing on me. I begin looking for a twig, anything that I can use to flick it away, when Uda opens his eyes. Our gazes meet, and I feel something move from him to me, almost like an electrical current. He raises his head towards the treetop where B'ma is perched and makes a clicking sound like one of the omnipresent green lizards. Immediately B'ma begins drawing something hand over hand.

Now I can see what he's pulling. It's a fine, threadlike cord. He is pulling it from the other side of the chasm. In a short time the thread thickens to become a cord, then a short time later, a rope. B'ma passes the rope to Masamo and descends the rest of the way to the ground.

Ete and Sua pick me up. I make one nervous glance at the spot where I'd last seen the spider. What if it jumped on me while I was looking away? Then we are out in the open. I am dumped on the ground just where the finger of rock joins the wide level shelf. Uda has taken a bow and arrow and stands watching the forest to my left apprehensively. He is poised on the balls of his feet, his head slowly turning as he searches for any movement. I have no doubt that he knows exactly what to do with the weapon.

B'ma and Sua run out to the end of the finger of rock and join the team on the rope, which now splits into two at a Y junction. The four are heaving in unison, pulling in two feet at a time. I see a three-sided rope bridge break loose from the foliage on the other side. It's what I feared. It's doubtless the bridge Masamo saw in his dream. Now things begin moving very fast, while they seem in some strange way to slow down. It's a curious phenomenon, one I know well from combat.

I can hear noises, still far in the distance. Noises of pursuit. The bridge begins to reach across the chasm. It's about four feet high, roughly triangular in shape. Two heavy ropes of vine are attached by connecting loops to a third wide rope of vine that forms a kind of floor. I cannot believe I am going to be carried across on that thing. I am sweating like a pig. The four are beginning to strain at the effort of pulling the bridge across. My shoulders and arms tense along with each drag. If I could get out of this damn carrier for just a few minutes to help it would go twice as fast. I'm aching with the strain and frustration of my inactivity.

Now there is a mighty pull from everyone and the bridge reaches the projecting finger of stone. B'ma shouts something, and Masamo practically flies up into the tree where he and B'ma were waiting earlier, carrying the lines with him. He begins to lash the two top lines to the trunk, while Sua and Ete are making the two lower lines fast around a boulder close to where I have been dumped. I can see that the bottom vine of the bridge is actually two separate ropes with small strips of bamboo lashed between them, making a floor about five inches wide to walk on. The whole thing is impossibly flimsy. I cannot imagine that anyone can cross it, much less two men carrying me at the same time.

The sounds of pursuit are closer. Uda shouts something to B'ma, who is waiting at the end of the bridge. B'ma yells back and points in the direction of the sound, but Uda shouts the same thing again. This time B'ma springs onto the bridge and starts across, although he keeps stopping to look back over his shoulder. Uda shouts again, and now B'ma fairly dances across. I am somewhat relieved by his quick transit, although he is a real lightweight, maybe weighing sixty pounds, and as agile as a monkey.

Masamo runs to Uda and takes the bow and arrow. He has a full quiver of arrows on his back. His blowpipe is left at the bank end of the finger of rock. Uda now crosses the vine bridge behind B'ma. As soon as he reaches the far side, Sua and Ete pick up my carrier. At the first step onto the bridge, I feel Sua slip. He has the bamboo pole balanced on his right shoulder, while he grabs the hand rope with his left hand. There is a grunt from Ete as he strains to hold me steady while Sua regains his balance. Ete still stands on solid ground. Masamo has now moved closer to the point of crossing, although he stands on the other side of the boulder to which the lines are lashed. I swear that I hear him say to the others, "Steady, slow down," although, of course, he is speaking S'norran.

86

I am being carried headfirst across the chasm. I make no attempt to look down. The further bank is a foot or two higher than the side we are leaving, so my head is high enough to give me a clear view behind us. Ete's face is oddly calm. His eyes seems unfocused. He does not look at me or down at his feet, but keeps his gaze resting on what I assume is the far bank. I realize that he is in a trancelike state.

We are almost a third of the way across when Heeta appears out of the forest to my left. He takes in the situation at a glance and waves a signal of some kind to Masamo, who moves to the bridge side of the boulder. Heeta steps back under cover, and immediately one of "the fools" appears where Heeta stood only a moment ago. Masamo has picked up the blowpipe, and with a single blow puts a dart neatly into the man's chest. The man does not drop to the ground immediately, but staggers and falls back into the cover of the trees. Now Heeta breaks from where he was concealed and makes a run for the gigantic tree to which the top lines are attached. Four of "the fools" step out from the woods, but quickly fall back when Masamo sends another dart in their direction, striking one of them in the calf.

The bridge is swaying wildly. I can hear Sua's rasping breath as he pants with the effort of balancing my weight with so little support. There is a word from Ete, and our slow crawl is stopped. We have gone a little less than halfway. Now two of "the fools" step out and send arrows towards Masamo, while another two appear on the far right. Heeta shoots at the two on the right and then dashes for the boulder. This time "the fools" hold their ground, and an arrow hits Heeta in his left shoulder. I see him reach back and pluck it out before he sends two arrows quickly in the direction it came from.

We begin to move again, more slowly, controlling the sway at each step. Masamo is at the end of the bridge now, unprotected by the mass of the boulder. However, the two "fools" on the right do not attack, but instead begin to climb the tree where the top lines are attached. Heeta yells a warning at Masamo, who quickly raises his blowpipe and shoots a dart at one of "the fools." It misses. He shoots again, while Heeta keeps "the fools" who are massing on the left at bay. The second dart finds its target, and one of "the fools" in the tree screams out and drops to the ground. As quickly as he is down, however, another one begins climbing to where the lines are tied.

I can see that the first man in the tree is successfully loosening the left hand line. "The hand line is going!" I yell. Sua and Ete stop, and Ete glances behind. He says a few words in S'norran, and Sua somehow manages to switch the bamboo pole to his left shoulder and grab the hand line on the right just as the left goes slack. I can only assume that Ete has managed the same maneuver, as we only pause for a moment in our slow progress. Now the left hand line is hanging loosely about halfway down to the foot rope. With each step, the bridge sways dangerously. We still have a fourth of the way to go. "The fools" are advancing on Heeta's position. Masamo is crouched at the end of the bridge, and now begins moving across backwards. He takes a step or two, steadies himself against the one hand line and then swiftly lets an arrow fly, catching himself and righting his balance again before he takes another step backwards. Heeta is still positioned behind the boulder. He has hit one of the men in the tree with an arrow, but he has been hit again himself in the left side. This time he does not pull the arrow out, but continues his steady firing.

We are almost across. I can hear Uda's voice on the bank ahead. He is speaking in a deep, strong voice, almost chanting. Our pace quickens. I can't tell how much further we have to go. Masamo is almost halfway across himself now. There is a shout from Heeta, and I see that one of "the fools" has successfully made his way up the tree on the far side of the trunk, safe from Heeta's arrows. The second hand line is about to go.

For a moment we seem to move very rapidly, almost flying the next few steps. I can see Heeta, still guarding the lines at the boulder, although so many arrows protrude from him by now that he looks like a pincushion.

Masamo has dropped to the floor of the bridge and is wrapping his arms and legs around the narrow span of the bottom vines. There is a shout from behind me as Uda reaches forward to drag Ete and the end of my hammock to solid ground. At the same moment the second hand line drops, but Sua manages to shove the pole forward and then leap to safety himself. I can see Masamo slowly inching his way along the bottom vines.

Now all of our eyes are on Heeta. He turns to looks at us, and for a moment, outlined against the brilliant light of the day, he seems huge. Arrows stick from his sides, his arms, his buttocks, his thighs. He abandons the boulder completely. "The fools" ignore him now and race to the boulder, quickly working the lines loose.

We watch Heeta, who slowly and majestically moves to the middle of the finger of stone. He stands for a moment, then extends his arms wide and leaps out into space in a magnificent swan dive. I see him leap, arch, and then—stranger than strange—he seems to separate into two forms. At first I can hardly believe my eyes. One of the forms, bristling with arrows, completes the dive, plummeting, soundlessly, head-first into the chasm below. The other form, however, is completely free of arrows. This other body seems to lift free from the first, climbing, higher and higher, freer and freer, into the potent blue of the sky—until it disappears from sight.

There is a victorious shout from the other side as one of the lines is pulled loose from the boulder. Masamo is still twenty feet from the bank. Before he can climb to safety, "the fools" untie the final line. The lines slide away from the far side of the bank and the entire bridge falls free, collapsing into the chasm, Masamo clinging to the bottom vines.

Only moments later, when the bridge stops swinging and is finally still, resting against the wall on our side of the crossing, Masamo quickly climbs the rest of the way to safety.

❧ 18 ❧

BEFORE I HAD TIME TO CATCH MY BREATH, TWO MEN STEPPED out from the cover of the trees and picked up my carrier, which Ete and Sua had dropped to the ground ten feet from the edge of the chasm. Without a word to the others, they drew me back into the forest, moving rapidly along a narrow path. I was too startled to cry out at first. I think I was still too shocked and shaken by the preceding events to have my wits about me. Finally I yelled out a couple of times, calling Uda and then all the other names as loudly as I could manage from such an exquisitely uncomfortable position. When the carrier was thrown up onto the bank from the bridge, I had become turned in my hammock and was now facedown, my legs and butt twisted uncomfortably beneath me. I couldn't see the men who were racing along with me, and it was difficult to make much noise from that position.

In only a few moments, however, I was dropped to the ground again, this time hitting my still sensitive right leg in a way that produced the most excruciating pain, and the men disappeared in the direction we had come from. I immediately began trying to shift my position so that I could loosen the netting and escape from my bonds. The bamboo pole was threaded through the edges of the hammock, then reinforced again with additional lashings. I thought I could release the tension, then slide the bamboo out, and free myself. I managed to turn around enough to get my hand on the bamboo and start the slow, laborious process of shoving the pole through the lashings. It was hot work, and confined as I was in the hammock, I could only manage a few inches at a time. I stopped for a moment to listen—surely I would hear some noise if the two men were attacking my companions—but all was quiet. I went back to my chore, now using my left hand as well, although the lacy cast around my left shoulder kept movement on that side to a minimum.

I finally managed to force the pole far enough along to free a foot or so of netting, maybe enough for me to crawl out. I began struggling to work myself out of the hammock, at the same time breaking loose the vines that bound my crutch to the pole. I wouldn't get far without it. Then I heard the noises. They were coming back.

I made a final monumental effort and rolled free, wrenching my crutch loose at the last minute. I struggled to my feet, throwing a quick glance behind me to see if I had been discovered. B'ma burst into view on the narrow path we had traveled, waving vigorously, beaming joyously.

"Keeltee! Holy cow, Keeltee!"

"B'ma!" What in the hell was going on? Behind B'ma were the two strange men, gently cradling Masamo in their arms, while they smiled at me with wide grins, revealing brilliant white teeth. Uda was immediately behind them.

Uda gave me a quick wave, which I interpreted to mean, "Not now," and dropped to the ground next to Masamo, whom the two men had placed carefully down, laying him on his right side. Now I could see the shaft of an arrow protruding from his left thigh. The arrowhead was buried in the flesh, the shaft broken off at about five inches. Uda leaned down, smelling around the wound. He asked Masamo some question, then bent closer and carefully smelled Masamo's breath. Next he swung his carrying basket around and very, very cautiously removed the top layer of padding that protected the remaining detonators. When they were unpacked and safely stored behind him, he drew out a leaf envelope, opening it to reveal a series of folded packets. He smelled each of them, selected two from the group, and opened them. He closed his eyes and sat completely silent for a minute or two. Then he smelled the wound again, then each of the parcels. He placed one in front of him and closed his eyes again for a moment. When he opened his eyes he gestured to Sua, who knelt beside Masamo.

Uda spoke a single word to Masamo, sharp, like a command, and instantly Sua grabbed the broken shaft of the arrow, drawing it from Masamo's thigh with a single, powerful pull. Uda immediately poured a third of the contents of the packet on the wound, then added juice from a fleshy leaf that Ete handed him. Finally, he dabbed a tiny portion of the contents on Masamo's tongue. Masamo swished the substance around his mouth for a moment, then nodded his agreement, and swallowed.

When Masamo swallowed, it was as if a sigh of relief rose from everyone. I could feel tension ebbing, like a threatening storm had passed. Uda carefully refolded the packets and returned them to the leaf envelope. Now he looked at me.

"Fools still using old poisons, Keeltee. Antidote works. Masamo okay now."

I looked at Masamo. His smooth, dark apricot skin had a dusky shadow on it, like the violet bloom of grapes. His eyes were closed and he breathed in short, rasping breaths, his chest rising and falling as if he were under extreme stress. He didn't look okay to me.

Buteh and Along (whom I privately thought of as Curly and Moe) had arrived from the main group just as Ete and Sua threw themselves, and me, onto the bank from the vine bridge. Fearing that the arrows or darts of "the fools" had the capability of reaching across the chasm, they lost no time in carrying me to the safety of the forest, even though I thought I was being kidnapped. I asked Uda how they knew we were coming, feeling sure the answer would be the usual "Because we are the people of the dream." This time, however, Uda gave me a more interesting reply. He told me that B'ma "telephoned" them last night when he was asleep. Actually, he said something like: "Keeltee, you want to tell someone you come, yes? You pick up farspeaker, yes? Make call." It took me a minute to work out what "farspeaker" was, then I nodded.

"Good system," he said. "Works. But costs, too, yes?" I nodded again. "Breaks down, yes?" I agreed. He went on. "S'norra system good, too, but no wires, doesn't break down. Last night B'ma visits Anjang, says we come. Anjang sends Along and Buteh. Here they are."

I thought for a minute. Seemed like a pretty good system to me, actually, but I still had some questions. I tried to frame my major problem with the method. What made it even harder, was that even though I found it to be conceptually impossible, I seemed to be experiencing the method almost every night.

"How does he do it, Uda? How does B'ma visit Anjang at night—or whenever?"

"Think of Anjang, Keeltee. Close eyes and think of Anjang now."

Obediently I closed my eyes and brought to mind a picture of the most gloriously beautiful woman I had ever seen. Easy. I opened my eyes.

"See Anjang, Keeltee?"

"Sure."

He didn't reply. I looked at him for a minute. "I thought of her. I imagined her, Uda—but I didn't go there. I didn't visit her, and I don't think I gave her a message."

"Okay. One minute." Now he was in full turtle. "You awake, Keeltee." He pinched me hard. "Yes? You are awake. You are here. Dreamtime you are everywhere. Body sleeps. You go."

I was ready to protest and question further when I remembered what I had seen. I reached forward, touching Uda very gently on the shoulder.

"Uda? When Heeta dove from the rock outcropping?"

He looked at me with undisguised interest.

"Yes, Keeltee."

"I saw something. I thought I saw something . . ." I corrected. He waited, a small smile forming on his lips. "I saw him dive. His body dropped into the chasm. But some other part . . . something lifted away. No arrows. It lifted into the sky." Now we were both quiet.

Uda finally broke the silence. "Heeta good dream flyer. Going home."

"Heeta was dead, Uda."

"Yes, completely dead forever. Before only half dead."

I closed my eyes and shook my head. Just when I think I'm getting the story, the whole thing shifts again.

"I don't get it, Uda. Heeta was a powerful, strong, healthy man. He wasn't sick. Nothing was wrong. How can you say he was half dead? You said I was part dead when you pulled me from the plane, but I was injured, badly injured. Nothing was wrong with Heeta."

Uda tapped my palm very softly with his light fingers, just as he had on that first night I was conscious in the hut. "Before we come to find you, Keeltee, Heeta has great dream. Going home dream. Finishes his dream story. No problem. All say good-bye to Heeta. We cry, dance, sing, eat. Big good-bye. Then we leave to find you. Every night while we travel Heeta goes home again, but comes back in the morning. Body is waiting. Now body is gone. Heeta is completely dead forever."

I can't get this one at all. "He was killed, Uda. He was full of poisoned arrows, and he jumped off a cliff. I saw it."

"Body not important, Keeltee. Don't need to kill body to die. You saw Heeta fly home."

I decided to give it one last shot. "Okay. So Heeta went home every night while we were traveling. That means he went to the place where all the dead people are, right?"

Uda pursed his lips thoughtfully. "All not home. Your men on their way maybe. Some never get home."

"But basically he went there every night." Uda nodded. "How did he know it was time to stay there? Didn't he go because his body was shot full of arrows? That's how it looked to me."

"Keeltee, sometimes you visit friends who live in big, wonderful place. Happy place. You like it very much, but you still go back to own house, yes? Maybe you have some work, yes? But jolly good to visit old friends in beautiful place. Then sometime you are tired, work is finished, house worn out. Maybe you can't do more. You go to sleep and visit friends in beautiful place. They say, stay here with us, Keeltee. Stay in good place now. Oh, you say, yes maybe, maybe not. You go back home. But now you keep thinking about beautiful place with old friends. Maybe your dream is finished. One night you go to sleep. Don't wake up. You go home to stay."

I didn't quite get it. But it was sure an interesting way to think about death. Uda was beaming at me, so I nodded as if I understood, although I still felt like I was missing some important piece of information.

19

WE RESTED FOR A DAY AND NIGHT AT THE CAMP ALONG AND
Buteh had prepared a short distance away. They continue to
remind me of Curly and Moe, or is it Larry and Moe? Never
could remember which of the Three Stooges was which.
Along's high brow is framed by tufts of thick, curly hair of
reddish bronze, which sticks out at the sides. None of the
S'norra are bald. His facial expression is one of constant
amazement, while Buteh, whose brow is low, has a hairline
shaped in that square-cut Prince Valiant style, and seems to
be in perennial doubt. Together, they're quite a pair.

To my considerable surprise, Masamo recovered rapidly
from the effects of the poison, and by morning seemed quite
strong. Anjang did not visit me. I had complicated dreams
of crashing through the jungle pursued by an unidentified
something. When Uda translated for me at our morning
dream circle, B'ma offered the suggestion that I turn around
next time and find out what the something wanted as it
probably needed my help. He's quite a guy, that kid. I took
his suggestion to heart and told him thank you, that I would
try next time.

No one was quite satisfied by my answer. I was surprised, to tell the truth, because I've been trying to get the
dream thing right so we can all move on. There was silence
until B'ma spoke up again. This time he told me that it was

sometimes good to call for an ally when confronting something that was after you, even something that only wanted your help. He said he would be glad to come at night into my dream if I called for him. I nodded. Now everyone seemed content, and we moved on.

All the others, including Uda, reported long dreams that seem to do with the violence of the previous day. There was a lot of discussion and comparing of notes. Apparently everyone has to be cleansed or released in some way before we can go back to the main group. I guess we will stay another night to be sure.

While the others were reporting their dreams, I'm ashamed to say I listened in a kind of jealous agony to hear if Anjang's name was mentioned. I was afraid that she didn't visit me because she was "healing" the others. I was vastly relieved when I didn't hear her name spoken by anyone.

We seem to have returned to Eden. I can't think of any other way to adequately describe the beauties of this place. Above us tower the peaks of the divide. Some parts are always covered with a delicate mist that drifts down into the narrow valleys and rifts of the mountains. It will clear for a moment, revealing a spectacular waterfall, then close again, so that your eye is constantly drawn from one vista to another. In some ways the lushness of the landscape reminds me of old growth forest up the McKenzie River. I've camped there all of my life. It's one of the most magnificent places in the world. But there's a major difference. Even in deep summer up the McKenzie, there's a hint of the winter to come. Sometimes the temperature drops to 38 degrees on an early morning in August. The most fragile fern will have to survive months of snow cover.

This world has a more gentle nature. The ground is soft underfoot, with a thick carpet of brownish moss, running with tiny streams of amber water. I have seen pitcher plants and clumps of yellow and white flowers resembling the trilliums that grow in the Oregon mountains. And the orchids are everywhere! My mother would think she'd died and gone to heaven if she saw them. Most grow on trees, somehow choosing exactly the right spot so their mass of color is directly under the rays of sunlight filtering down through the leaves overhead. In the darkness of the forest it's like a spotlight shining on them. They are all shapes, all sizes, with colors and patterns I can't begin to describe, one a purple that is almost black, another a mottled black and green marked exactly like a toad's back.

I took a stroll up the trail, with B'ma along in case I got into trouble. Actually it was more like a stagger as the end of my crutch kept sinking into the mossy ground and throwing me off balance. We still had a great time pointing things out to each other, oohing and aahing. We reached a place where a tree right out of *Swiss Family Robinson* straddled the path. It was something. Must have been two hundred feet high or more, with a system of massive, buttressed trunks. The trail passed right through the tree. Later when we got back, I learned from Uda that it's a favorite place to hide if some wild boar has got your scent and is pursuing you down the path.

B'ma and I were sitting down to rest under one of the arches formed by the roots that rise so magnificently when he gestured for quiet. Instantly he was perfectly silent, perfectly still. I did my best to copy him exactly. Then I heard a dry cough not too far away. B'ma's eyes widened for a moment.

We were barely breathing. Another cough, this time further away. Then another, still further. He still wouldn't let me get up to head back to the others for a good bit of time. When we returned he very excitedly reported our adventure to Uda. Then I learned that the dry cough is the undeniable signal of a leopard. Boy, did I get a chill when I heard that. Sure won't forget that sound for a while. Can't help thinking I would have liked to see it, but maybe I'll have a chance under less vulnerable circumstances.

Uda says tomorrow we will visit a place of healing where strong smelling hot water springs from the ground. Apparently it's a great place to soak wounds. Must be a natural sulfur springs.

20

November 1, 1944

It's only a few days since my last entry, but it seems like weeks. Those few days have been action packed! We're resting again, so I have some time to catch up. I've had a couple of very interesting conversations with Uda that I want to record. But first, there are two lines of poetry that keep running through my head, from "Hiawatha," by Longfellow, I think. "This is the forest primeval/ The home of the pines and the hemlock." I'm sure he was describing the East Coast of America when it was still Indian territory, but it sure hits the feeling I have that I'm in the first place, the "forest primeval." I wish I remembered more poetry. I don't think my descriptions do this glorious landscape justice. A little inner voice keeps saying to me, "This is how it was at the beginning of things." I feel awed, as if I were in a holy place with holy people. Is this what it means to "go native"? If it is, then more of us ought to do it.

We're at a natural hot springs—sulfur, as I suspected. It's pretty dramatic. Suddenly you step out of dense forest onto a vast stretch of rock, completely exposed to the full force of the sun. Water bubbles out at several different points, boiling hot and smelling like Lucifer's bathtub. As the water trickles down the rock fault, it meanders along, forming pools of different depths and temperatures, finally joining another stream of very cool water at the bottom of the rocks. It's an amazing tonic. I started at the bottom and gradually worked my way up to the hotter pools, but even then I couldn't stay in near as long as the others.

The cool water at the bottom forms a magical pool just inside the shade of the trees. Surrounding this pool are small plants, about the size of trilliums and with similar foliage, but with blossoms that look like small pink pine cones standing upright. B'ma showed me how to squeeze the flower, which then exudes a clear juice used as a shampoo and body soap. It's really great, smells a little like ginger beer. I have to admit I tasted some to test it. Soapy. No surprise.

I've also been encouraged to drink quantities of the sulfur water. So far it's given me a colossal case of the farts, and I suspect the runs are close behind (no pun intended).

We will return to our camp before dusk. Uda tells me that animals gather here in the cool of the evening to drink and bathe. He showed me tracks of deer, wild pigs, leopards, tiger, and a couple of other things that I don't recognize. Apparently game gathers here from miles around, but the S'norra don't hunt them while they're at the springs. Not many days ago I wouldn't have understood why. Now it seems to make sense to me.

I had been thinking about something Uda said when we were discussing Heeta's death. He said that Heeta had "finished his dream story." What triggered my memory was Along's report this morning in the dream circle. He was describing last night's dream, and Ete asked him a question relating to "his dream story." Animated discussion followed. Uda only translated a word here and there, so I couldn't get most of it. So today, while we were lazing around one of the lukewarm pools, I asked him if everyone had "a dream story." He said, "Of course." I asked how you knew what your dream story was.

He was thoughtful for a bit. Sometimes I get the feeling that a question I ask is quite horrifying to him, as if it reveals a serious lack of education or culture on my part. It's almost as if he's shocked to learn that I don't know or understand certain essential things. This was one of those times.

"First remembered dream very important, Keeltee," he said. "Tells story of life. How can you know when it's time to go home if you don't know your dream story?"

You can bet I didn't have an answer to that one. I tried again.

"I'd like to know these things, Uda. How can I find out what my dream story is?" Now he was pleased.

"When you are little boy, Keeltee, big dream comes. Maybe you don't write it down. Maybe you don't write at all yet. But it stays in your head and you remember."

Well, I didn't remember, to tell the truth, but I almost do. It's like a distant echo. You know what it's like trying to remember the name of the towheaded kid you sat next to all through the second grade? You can remember the exact color of his thick hair and his slightly sour, musty smell—but not his name. I'm close though. I think I'll be able to get it. But I had another question for Uda.

"This messenger business?" That got his full attention immedi-ately. "Let's just say that I am the messenger." Uda nodded. He has never evidenced a moment's doubt from the beginning. "Can you tell me what the messenger is expected to do?"

He gave me a deep look. "No worry, Keeltee. You will know."

"Do you know, Uda?"

He didn't answer immediately, but stood and moved to the edge of the water, gazing into it for quite a long time. Then he rejoined me where I was propped against some rocks in the shade of an overhang.

He looked at me for a bit. It was not a searching look, by any means, but I felt him looking into me in some way. He answered. "Yes."

"Tell me." He continued to hold my gaze. I had tried to keep any note of pleading out of my voice. If I knew what the messenger was supposed to do, I thought, at least I could assess my capacity to fulfill the S'norran expectations. Uda apparently didn't agree.

His answer was simple. "No."

Nevertheless, I felt a little relieved. At least someone knew, even if it wasn't me.

21

WE'VE SPENT ALL MORNING PRIMPING. THERE'S NO OTHER word for it. The camp looks like a big beauty shop. Yesterday everyone washed their loincloths in the hot springs, and there was a lot of hair plucking and general cleaning up, but that was nothing compared to our preparations today. I'm beginning to feel like a bridegroom just before his wedding.

In fact, it did occur to me that when Uda says everyone must agree first and then there'll be a ceremony—before I can laugh with Anjang—that he might be talking marriage. At first I was shocked. I guess I have more prejudices than I realized. I thought about bringing Anjang home to Eugene to meet my folks. There are a couple of Jewish families in town. Rubensteins own the big furniture store, and my Mom plays bridge every week with Mrs. Rubenstein and the Happy Dozen Club. A couple of Jewish kids went to school with me. Several Italian families moved to Eugene a few years ago, too, but I didn't know the kids. They all went to Catholic school. I'd never seen a Negro in the flesh, just in movies, until the military. I have a lot of respect for a man like Jesse Owens, of course, but I immediately wondered if people in Eugene, Oregon, would think of Anjang as a colored woman?

My folks'll hack me—I know that. Anyway, I've decided that I'll do it, and the devil take the hindmost, as my grandfather used to say. I realize, of course, that a jungle wedding wouldn't hold up in an American court of law, but that's not the issue for me. When I make a commitment, it's real. And if Anjang will have me, I'm ready to make the commitment. I can't imagine another girl anywhere in the world with such grace and loveliness, such strength, such beauty, such dignity. I will be proud to introduce her as my wife.

The word "wife" gives me the jitters.

I have refused to be carried into the main camp in my hammock, which was a great disappointment to Ete and Sua, and to B'ma, who were planning elaborate decorations for the carrier. I don't want Anjang's first glimpse of me to be in that thing. So attention has been turned to my crutch, which now has carved decorations running up and down its length and tufts of multicolored feathers sticking out the top. That's nothing compared to our personal makeup. B'ma has been painted to look like a leopard. It's fantastic. Once again he produced pots of colored goop, a kind of ocher white, thick, pasty stuff, and some dense black. Everyone else will be painted mostly white. I'll be decorated with the black and a few white highlights. I was quite surprised by the total seriousness of our preparations. Everyone's really lighthearted, as usual, but it's clear that getting ready for our triumphal entry is a matter of some importance.

B'ma is quite gorgeous, painted all over with complex whorls and spots. I asked Uda if the leopard represented a totem animal for his family or the tribe. Uda considered this for a moment and then said something to B'ma, who replied that he wanted to look like a leopard to scare the other children! I don't know a whole lot about anthropology, but I do know something about the traditions of the West Coast Indian tribes. The Warm Springs Indians still came to the ranch to pick hops every year when I was a boy. The S'norra don't seem to have similar beliefs at all.

Uda is resplendent in a fine fur hat made from a civet cat, shaped almost like an aviator's cap, but with orchid blossoms sticking out from the ear holes. Pretty nifty. I am certainly the pièce de résistance, as the French say, as I have been turned into a walking tartan, black and white and plaid all over. In addition to which I am crowned with an orchid wreath, big yellow blossoms alternating with the deep purple blooms, which B'ma says are particularly fetching with my dark hair—or words to that effect.

Everyone has helped everyone else get ready, and a fine company of bucks we are. I only wish I had a camera to preserve the sight, especially Along's very large, muscular buttocks, which are enhanced with a couple of bull's eyes, alternating black and white circles. Fraternity hazing was nothing compared to this. Now that I think about it, that's a stupid comparison. The purpose of fraternity hazing was always humiliation. Camaraderie forcibly imposed through shared suffering. This is something else completely.

I've been cautioned not to move around too much in my hammock, for fear of smearing my plaid. I'm practically rigid anyway, anticipating what it's going to be like. We stopped just before the clearing to organize the parade. B'ma will step out into the open space first, followed by Uda and then me. The others are arrayed behind us. Even the long blowpipes have had their ends stuffed with flowers and trailing vines. Portland Rose Parade, here we come!

I could see past Uda and over B'ma's head. There, in the full sunlight, stood Anjang. I lost my breath for a moment at the sight of her. She was not so tall as she has seemed in my dreams, but even more gloriously lovely. The light of the sun seemed to collect around her. A garland of deep red orchids crowned her head, and long, trailing ropes of glistening green leaves encircled her neck, through which her firm, completely bare breasts thrust themselves boldly forward. When I saw those rosy, brown nipples, I confess I staggered and almost fell to the ground. In my dreams she was always decorously enclosed in a wrap like Uda's, covering her from armpits to mid-calf.

B'ma ran forward, forgetting for a moment that he was a terrifying leopard man, and threw himself at Anjang's knees. She leaned down, taking his face in her hands, and kissed him very gently and lovingly, then removed one of the green garlands and placed it around his neck. B'ma began pulling on her hand, dragging her over to me. I had stepped forward behind Uda, but found myself quite overwhelmed by shyness. I had prepared a line of greeting in S'norran, coached by Uda and B'ma, but the words left me. I was speechless with excitement, undone by the intensity of my feeling.

Then she was in front of me, raising her eyes to meet mine. Her look was so gentle, so infinitely tender. She lifted one of the garlands from her neck as I leaned down so she could place it around mine. I ached to throw my arms around her and lift her to me in a passionate embrace, but I restrained my impulse. She gravely kissed me on both cheeks, just as she had welcomed my men in the USO, and stepped back.

Now the others came forward. As I watched, Masamo ran ahead to greet Anjang. Without waiting for her to place a garland on his neck, he grabbed her around the waist and raised her to him, kissing her passionately and thoroughly.

B'ma ran back to them both, and the three drew themselves together into one unit. Suddenly I understood. I saw the truth. I staggered beneath a realization so overwhelming to me that I didn't know if I could endure it. Anjang is Masamo's wife. B'ma is their child.

ᵃᵃ 22 ᵃᵃ

I DON'T KNOW HOW I GOT THROUGH THE REST OF THE DAY. Something broke in me. I guess my heart. Uda stepped next to me immediately after Masamo's embrace of Anjang. "Keeltee?" I turned to him with undisguised agony. I don't know if he understood completely, but he quickly gestured to someone and I was provided with a mat, where I sprawled rather indecorously, I'm afraid. There was a procession of S'norra with wreaths and garlands for me. I did my best to regain some degree of composure, but I could barely function. I don't remember much of it.

After a time, whether long or short, it was impossible for me to say, things slowed down, and I was taken to the longhouse to rest while everyone else concentrated on preparations for the night's feast. The longhouse was about sixty feet long, raised on stilts. I wasn't sure I could manage the bamboo ladder with my bum leg, but I managed to pull myself up, mainly with the strength of my arms. I found myself in a space divided into separate cubicles, separated from each other by matting partitions about four feet high. I was led to a raised platform at the end, a kind of guest room, I take it. I think I was in shock. Every image seemed surreal to me, colors were abnormally bright, angles seemed acute, no soft edges anywhere. I looked at everything with extreme interest, as if my life depended on noting exact details. I was trying with all of my might not to think. Not to remember. Not to know.

I carefully counted eleven compartments, plus the platform at the end. Some of the cubicles seemed unused. Others were furnished with sleeping mats, and the compartments along the walls next to them held foodstuffs and other containers. Possessions were stored on the rafters above the cubicles. I felt a tremor as I passed one of the sections. I immediately assumed it was the space normally occupied by Anjang and her family. I felt as if my skin had been flayed. I was sensitive to such a degree that I feared I'd burst into tears. I've got to get hold of myself, I thought.

I didn't know if I could stand it. I was afraid I would start screaming in rage at what seemed a colossal betrayal. But who had betrayed me?

Everyone.

I would imagine racing out to the compound and venting my anger at all of the S'norra. How dare they? Then I would plan a chilling revenge. I would disappear during the night with no explanation, leaving them to work out what had offended the long-awaited messenger. They would be sorry. They would all be very, very sorry.

By the time Sua and Ete were sent to collect me for the evening's events, I had fortunately progressed beyond this stage of agitation and was able to evidence a kind of false calm. I have almost no memory of the celebration other than a brief few minutes of reprieve.

In the midst of the feast I was ceremonially led to a small hut, like the ones we camped in during our journey. Several of us sat under a leafy porch sheltering the doorway while Uda went inside. Shortly he reappeared and gestured for me to follow him. I managed to hobble in and sit on a mat to one side. A small fire glowed on a center platform of packed earth. Fragrant smoke spiraled to the roof of the hut, where it dissipated through spaces between the leaves. It took a few moments for my eyes to adjust to the dim light.

Directly across from me sat two wizened creatures of blackened skin and visible bone. It crossed my mind that the couple might be actual mummies. Then the figure on the right moved, turning to look at me with eyes that already had a bluish film over them. When I looked directly into those eyes I was flooded by something so extraordinary that all of my grief and rage, for a few moments anyway, faded into nothing. Tears began to run down my face, but they were the tears that come when there is nothing possible to say. I heard Uda speak in S'norran. He translated for me: "I have told Ata and Ada that messenger is here, Keeltee."

He gestured for me to move forward, closer to them. I did, sliding around the fire on my hands and knees, until I was directly in front of them. One at a time, each raised a bony hand and for a few seconds gently rested it on my head.

We left.

When we had returned to our places, Uda observed to me, "Ata and Ada mostly dead, long, longtime, Keeltee. Now they meet messenger, can go home for good."

I nodded weakly in response to this odd communication. He went on. "They are first ones, Keeltee. First S'norra came here to this place."

This was just too much for me. "What? You're telling me they're thousands of years old?"

Uda gave me a look of unreserved reproach. "Of course not. Come here. Go home. Come here. Go home. Over and over. Many, many times. Always together."

I couldn't take it. "This is crazy bullshit, Uda, and I don't think I can stand to hear any more of it."

He didn't reply to my outburst, but took my large, heavy hand in his small, strong one and held it tightly for some time.

23

SOMEHOW I MADE IT THROUGH THE EVENING. WHEN THE inevitable dancing got underway, I feigned weariness and got Ete and Sua to help me back up the ladder and into the longhouse. I hoped I could fall asleep and escape the emotional torrents raging through me. At first it worked. Then I woke up sometime before dawn, trying to get my bearings in the dense darkness of the night. The air was thick, damp and fragrant. I was sticky with sweat.

The entire building was vibrating, surging in a familiar, rhythmic motion. I could hear panting, moaning, and, yes, laughter. People were "laughing together" throughout the longhouse. I knew that two of those people were Masamo and Anjang. I stuffed my fingers in my ears. I gritted my teeth. With an enormous effort of will, I waited it out until dawn. When it was barely light enough to see and all was finally quiet, the building at last still, I grabbed my crutch, crawled across the springy floor to the entrance, and slid down the bamboo ladder, tossing my crutch out first. No matter what, I won't go back to the longhouse to sleep.

Now followed three of the most difficult weeks of my entire life. Uda agreed it was too strenuous for me to negotiate the ladder into the longhouse several times a day, so I was moved to a hut near the fields. The S'norra have cleared a small area where various crops are grown, apparently by burning the trees and undergrowth, as the area is covered with ash. A few huts have been thrown up between the jungle and the clearing, where young bachelors usually stay—like me, no doubt, driven mad by the nightly sounds of the more fortunate married men "laughing" with their wives. Water is conveniently near, as they have built a simple aqueduct system from a stream to the field by cutting out the nodes of split bamboo and overlapping the pieces on a raised framework. I am told one of the S'norra received the plan as "a gift" in a dream some time ago.

At first I thought I could simply avoid contact with Anjang. Once again I determined to make plans to return to my outfit as soon as I was physically able to travel. It occurred to me that one or two of the bachelors might be convinced to make a journey, providing me with the help I needed in exchange for which I would make sure they were amply rewarded when we reached our goal. Foolish as it seems, I managed to harbor this fantasy for some days. A major drawback, of course, was the fact that I could only communicate reliably with Uda—or Anjang. No one else spoke English. My vast vocabulary of S'norran was still limited to around a dozen words.

For a few days Uda came every morning to our dream circle, as I could not follow the reports or participate without his help. B'ma had moved out to the bachelor huts at the same time as me and was happy to spend his days showing me around and encouraging me to participate in the daily business of the group. No one seemed aware of my avoidance of Anjang, although I'm sure she must have noticed that I kept my distance whenever possible.

All together there appeared to be only about twenty-five S'norra in the entire compound, although I had learned there was another small group a short distance away, staying at one of the hunting camps. Most of the married couples were older than Anjang and Masamo. I had seen only one young girl, a few years older than B'ma. There was a single baby and one toddler, a cheery little fellow with curly, bright hair standing out from his head, much like Along's. For a few days I had thought there were a number of babies, but I eventually realized that a single baby was carried around and even nursed by several different women. I have been unable to determine who the actual parents of the toddler are, as he seems to be cared for by everyone in the camp.

I was not thinking about Anjang. My former discipline while overseas stood me in good stead, and as long as she was not physically present, I found I could stay in a somewhat comfortable frame of mind, at least while I was awake.

About a week after we arrived, Uda brought Anjang to the bachelor dream circle. No one else seemed surprised when she joined in with the others, listening to their dreams and commenting. However, instead of Uda translating for me, she began the task. I looked at Uda with surprise, but he only nodded and smiled. I'll have to admit that I was torn in two directions. I wanted to get up and run away as soon as I saw her coming, but another part of me would have done almost anything to keep her there as long as possible. Nevertheless, I was relieved when the circle was over and Anjang left, calling B'ma to join her at some chore.

Uda then drew me aside and explained that he and a few of the hunters were traveling to visit the other group, a day or two distant from us. I nodded, expecting that he might ask me to join them, as I was getting around much better, often not needing my crutch for an entire day. However, that was not the plan. He announced that he wished me to spend my days with Anjang, teaching her to speak better English, while I would also learn more S'norran. He added that he had taught her as much as he could.

I'll admit that my first thought was that I was being set up or tested in some way. Uda's face was blandly neutral, and he didn't seem to notice my discomfort.

It seems odd that I didn't question him at the time, but I believe I was restrained by fear. I was ashamed of my desire for a married woman, embarrassed by my earlier fantasy of marriage, of taking her to the States to meet my family and friends. I also carried a burden of anger. Somehow these people whom I had befriended and trusted had exposed me to the most terrible feeling of rejection of my entire life. I guess I felt that I had been used in some way. Shame is a funny thing. I found it easier to pretend that I was just fine, that I had never imagined that Anjang was my girl. I assumed that everyone else accepted my pretense, that no one noticed the extremity of my feeling.

"Is Masamo going with you?" I finally managed to stammer.

Uda gave me one of his deep looks. I had to drop my eyes. "No."

Again I felt a combination of relief and regret. Again I did my best not to acknowledge or recognize my own feelings.

That night I had the dream of being chased again. Actually, I'd been having it almost every night, but usually I could force myself to wake up before it got too bad. B'ma had been steadily reminding me to call for help, but to tell the truth, I wasn't very interested. He and the others had also recommended that I practice telling myself the story of the dream

120

when I was awake, calling for help, and then finding out what the pursuer wanted from me. I didn't do that either.

This time the dream was really terrifying. Whatever was after me was as dark and terrible as grim death. Somehow in the dream I knew that, try as I might, I could never escape. I managed to wake myself once again. I sat up with relief, thinking I would go outside and get some air. Even though I was alone in the hut, the atmosphere seemed stuffy and thick. Then I heard the sound outside. The beast was waiting for me. I could hear its snuffling breath against the fragile barrier of leaves, my only defense against the monster. Paralyzed with fear, greater than any I have ever known, I drew my bark cloth blanket over my head and cowered against the wall of leaves. My throat was frozen. I tried to cry out for help, but I could only make harsh gasps. I knew I was lost.

Then I woke up for real. The air was cool and soft, but my bark cloth blanket was soaked with perspiration. My heart was still racing from fear, and my chest ached from rough panting. I struggled up and managed to get outside, where I could sit with my back against one of the bamboo supports holding up the small verandah attached to my hut.

We studied some Freud in my beginning psych class in college, and I remembered that bad dreams were almost always about sex. In fact, most dreams were about sex, weren't they? I tried to apply my feeble little store of knowledge from the class to my dream. I thought to myself that I was pursued by the demon of lust. That seemed to fit. I didn't consider B'ma's remark that my pursuer might need something from me. What could I give to a demon of lust, anyway?

After a while I drank from the aqueduct and returned to bed.

☙ 24 ❧

THE NEXT MORNING ANJANG APPEARED AT OUR DREAM CIRCLE, explaining that Uda and the others had left for the hunting camp. I sat on a coco palm stump, turned so that I wasn't looking directly at her. It was easier that way.

Anjang listened to my dream report with a serious demeanor. I forgot my intent, leaning further and further forward so that I could see her. The early morning light rested with such grace on her features. The sunlight, breaking through the fingers of mist, seemed to catch in the dark mass of her honey-colored hair. She looked at me.

I fell forward, sprawling into the center of the circle. With what must have been a gargantuan effort of self-restraint, she didn't laugh at my clumsiness, nor did the others. As I was gathering myself up, B'ma talked for a bit. Anjang nodded, then spoke to me, this time without looking directly at me. "When B'ma small boy I tell him old story, story of children in jungle alone. He asks me to tell now. Good, Keeltee?"

Her voice was musical and low, her English, like Uda's, flavored with the most charming hint of British inflection. I would have happily listened to her recite the phone book.

She began with words that could have come from my own childhood storybook. "Long, longtime ago, deep in forest, two children living alone," the tale began. It was a story as familiar to me as "Jack and the Beanstalk." My mother loved fairy tales, and long after I pretended I was too old for such things, I used to listen to her read them to my little sister in the evenings when we were both in bed.

In Anjang's story, two children, a boy and a girl, live alone in a hut in the jungle, when a ferocious tiger begins prowling around their home. At first frightened, they discover that the tiger is hurt when they see the print of its paw. They decide they will put food out for it and so on and so on, and of course what happens is that the tiger befriends them and turns into a good spirit and grants them all kinds of boons, including leading them back to their family and tribe, from whom they've been separated for a long time.

I could have told it myself, after the first few minutes. It was "Snow White and Rose Red" with a few local twists, one of my sister's favorites. I'd heard it a dozen times. Of course, in the story my mother read, the bear had been bewitched, and could only turn back into a prince when one of the two girls overcame her fear and loved him. But I got the point. The funny thing is, when my mother read the story to my sister, I always thought of myself as the bear.

After Anjang finished, B'ma spoke again. She translated: "B'ma says most important, Keeltee. Tiger in dream or story, one thing. Tiger in jungle another. Do not feed or help tiger in jungle, yes?"

I had to smile at that. I assured B'ma I would remember the difference, and I promised that I would practice calling for help in my dream and finding out what the monster wanted from me. The funny thing is that my promise was genuine this time. I'm really going to do it. It doesn't mean that I've been converted to all this dream business, but I sure don't want to let B'ma down. He deserves better than that from me.

I spent the entire day, and most of every day for the next two weeks with Anjang.

It was tough.

I had thought of her as soft and curvy, like most of the girls back home. I quickly learned that she was as strong and agile as most men. What's more, she threw herself into physical labor with such gusto and good humor it seemed more like sport than work. In fact there's not much work that goes on here. The S'norra seem to survive, thrive even, without a lot of effort.

Food is easy to produce, as the soil is so rich. When the land is no longer fertile someone usually has a dream about a new site, so everyone moves there and helps build the new longhouse. It only takes a week for the group to build their new home, which lasts five or six years. It takes another week to clear a new planting area, although an additional area might be developed later on if someone has a dream about it. No more than a couple of hours a day are spent gathering or hunting food and working the fields.

Much of every day is spent discussing dreams or working on large dream projects. People are always working on new tools they saw in a dream or decorating something with patterns seen in a dream. The youngsters get help from everybody, putting together little dramas from dreams, with costumes and props, like plays in grade school.

When someone has a really important dream, everyone gathers after the small family circles and the entire group ponders the meaning of the big dream. Even the dream of a small child is accorded this importance. I believe Uda told me about it before, but I didn't really comprehend the significance until I experienced it. I think this is why B'ma has so much self-assurance and poise for such a young kid. It must be something to be taken seriously by adults and listened to with such attention.

Once I had asked Uda why the important dream wasn't reported to him. It seemed like a waste of time for everyone to listen and comment. He was quite startled by my question. Once again I had the feeling that I had revealed some extraordinary lack of education. I added hastily, "You're the chief, aren't you, Uda. Don't you make important decisions for the group? You're the one who keeps things in order."

He thought for a bit. "All voices important, Keeltee. Some old, speak soft, but wise. We listen. Heeta great hunter. All listen. Achok speak loud, so we listen. Big voice. If we listen, then Achok is quiet." He smiled at me. I got the picture. Achok was a deeply wrinkled woman with a habit of shaking her fingers at whomever she was addressing, usually at full volume. Everyone was quiet and listened attentively without interrupting when she spoke to the group.

Uda continued. "I travel far. See many things. So many listen. But no chief here, Keeltee. Many voices, no chief."

I thought he was finished and started to ask another question, but he raised a finger and I waited. "Voices of children most important, Keeltee. Children still close to home. Remember much."

I probably should have been satisfied by this, but I had another question. "What about disagreements, Uda. Let's say that someone is angry with someone else. Who decides what's right or wrong?"

He frowned at this. "Most important to get along with others, Keeltee. If disagree, then disagree with good humor."

So ended one of our many conversations on S'norran civics.

On a particularly difficult day towards the end of the three weeks, I was accompanying Anjang into the forest to cut special leaves to be used for repairing the thatch on one of the huts. B'ma was with us, and I followed the two of them, as usual failing to keep up with their rapid pace despite my efforts. I was also distracted by the vision of Anjang in front of me. Like everyone else, she wore only a loincloth, although she and several of the other women favored longer pieces of bark cloth, so that the ends waved alluringly when they moved. My attention was fixed on her lithe, athletic legs, the muscles of her smooth, round buttocks. I kept stumbling over unnoticed roots.

I was thinking hard about King Arthur. Actually I was thinking about Lancelot, never my favorite character in fiction. For the first time I was beginning to have some sympathy for him. Our situations were certainly different, but I was starting to see the point of the whole stupid story. It had seemed meaningless to me before. I had a naive belief in honor. I had always thought Lance was a jerk, and I dismissed his betrayal of Arthur and the Round Table as lack of discipline, some kind of weakness of character. Now I wasn't so sure.

Anjang and B'ma would stop to gather wild berries or fruits, waiting for me to catch up. It was a lighthearted pleasure trip, even though we had a task to perform. I had been invited along despite my clumsiness on the trail because my height would be an advantage in reaching the leaves, which grew high off the ground on the ends of tall stems.

When I caught up to them they were laughing at some shared joke. Anjang had stuck a brilliant scarlet flower behind one ear. It was a common practice among the S'norra to pick flowers and adorn your fellows. B'ma already wore a blossom at a rakish angle in his glossy curls. Anjang had to rise onto her toes to reach my ear, and as she did, she leaned forward so that her naked breasts ever so lightly brushed my chest. I felt as if I had been seared by lightning. She must have felt it, too, because there was a confused look in her eyes. I was glad B'ma was there. Anjang quickly drew back with a small frown and turned to continue along the narrow path.

There had been nothing flirtatious in any of our exchanges, no hint from her of the double messages that safely unavailable girls so often trailed behind them like perfume. Nevertheless, I believe it was at this moment that I made my decision.

I was not going to be dumb like Lancelot. No matter the temptation, I would contain my passion. I would treasure my love for Anjang, but never express it. It seemed to me that I could never love anyone else. So be it. If a life of celibacy and self-control was what God intended for me, I would handle it. I would be noble. Stumbling along, trying to avoid the thorny vines that can slice your skin right open, I made my vows, feeling like a knight of olden times. In fact, I was dumber than Lancelot had ever been.

25

I DON'T KNOW IF IT WAS MY NEWFOUND SAINTHOOD, ANJANG'S story, or what, but that night I cracked my dream.

It started, as usual, with me alone in the jungle. I was trotting along, enjoying myself—really enjoying myself. Everything seemed especially vivid; the colors were brilliant, the bird sounds particularly catchy. I could even smell things, good things. That's what changed first. I caught a whiff of something rank and stopped. At first I looked around, like I might see what smelled so bad. Then I heard it, or maybe felt it. Everything turned rotten, like a bad movie. The light changed, and color seemed to drain away so the shimmering greens of the foliage soured to a crud color while the sky turned dark and gray. I couldn't get enough air, and then I remembered.

There was a horror out there, and it was after me.

First I thought I would run, but my legs were heavy, like I could barely move them. The air got even more dense. I couldn't breathe.

Then I could hear the beast coming closer. I knew there was something I needed to remember.

Of course. I knew what it was. Uda had told me the Japs had terrible beasts of their own. That was it. The terrible Japanese beast. It wasn't after me at all. It was after the S'norra. I was safe from it.

I could breathe again. I exhaled with relief and stepped off the trail, secreting myself in the dense undergrowth alongside, secure in my knowledge that the beast would pass me by on its way to the S'norran compound.

The beast was approaching, its smell fetid, rank. I was very still.

It passed.

I sat for a moment, uncertain about my direction. Shouldn't the dream end now? Then a terrible thought came to me. The beast was after my friends—Uda, B'ma, and Anjang—the woman I was pledged to love forever, and all the others. They had no defense against such a monster. I had to protect them. I had to stop it.

Without a moment's hesitation, I stepped back into the middle of the trail, threw my head back, and did my very best imitation of Tarzan's jungle call, the sound echoing through the jungle in glorious dreamlike high fidelity.

Then I felt real terror. Somewhere, not too far away, I felt the evil presence sense the change in my attitude. I'd issued a challenge in no uncertain terms. The beast would return.

"Uda! B'ma!" I screamed. "I need your help now!"

I felt a light touch on my shoulder and turned. B'ma was there, in full leopard man paint, Uda next to him, complete with his civet cat bonnet. Just behind them was a brand shiny new galvanized iron garbage can with a lid on it. They dragged it to the center of the trail and pulled the lid off with a dramatic flourish.

The can was filled to the brim with dark honey. We melted into the shadowy underbrush to wait.

First the smell. Then the ground shaking at the heavy footfalls. I could see it—a cross between King Kong and a foul werewolf, huge, turning its great head and snuffling, smelling, seeking. It caught a whiff of the rich perfume coming from the garbage can. It hesitated for a brief second, an almost perplexed expression crossing its gross features.

Then it smiled. I saw it smile. The head disappeared as the beast buried its nose in the can.

I woke up. It was still the middle of the night. I felt lighter than air. I took a deep breath. The cool, sweet night air was like honey in my nostrils.

❧ 26 ❧

I HAD A HELL OF A TIME EXPLAINING THE SIGNIFICANCE OF Tarzan to everybody in the morning dream circle. The notion of "Lord of the Jungle" only mattered to me. The others were more concerned when I described how Tarzan and Jane lived alone, without a tribe to share their life. Nevertheless, it was clear to everyone that I had solved the problem of the beast, and I was warmly congratulated for the success of my device. I reminded them that it was Uda and B'ma who thought of the honey, not me. The major concern expressed was that I had forgotten to demand a gift from the beast once it was tamed. I suggested that he might appear in someone else's dream, who could collect it for me, an idea that wasn't received with much enthusiasm.

There's something quite satisfying about this dream business. Again I woke up this morning feeling like I'd taken care of some major problem. Nothing has really changed, in fact, but I feel like I'm different.

B'ma is teaching me to shoot with a bow and arrow. I've gotten pretty good with a fixed target, almost as good as he is. He still outranks me when the target is moving, or floating as the case may be. We spend time every day at the stream shooting at little leaf boats, then splashing into the water to fetch our arrows and cool off at the same time.

There don't seem to be any kids here B'ma's age. I asked Anjang if most of the children were with the hunting party at

133

the camp. She gazed at me as if she didn't quite understand my question. Then she shook her head. "No, children are here."

I guess I'm the first buddy B'ma's had. Obviously I'm a lot older, but when it comes to the basic skills the S'norra take for granted, I feel like a kid. I was a pretty serious Boy Scout for years, but some of the "skills" I won badges for seem silly compared to the things B'ma does. For example, I think I was about his age when I made a name plaque for my dad by gluing alphabet noodles onto a board and shellacking it. I've watched B'ma carve a complicated design on a bamboo flask with a sharpened stone and then grab a fiery stick from the campfire, using it to burn a complex and subtle design around his carving. A piece like that would sell for a lot back home, maybe even go into a museum.

B'ma and I returned from target practice one day to find Uda waiting beside the bachelors' fire. He seemed very pleased with himself. I started to sit on my palm stool, but instead he stood up and announced his intention to go fishing. I was surprised, as I'd assumed his party would bring back an abundance of game from the hunting group. It was unlike the S'norra to lay in more food than was necessary for a day or two. Nevertheless, Uda briskly rose and started back towards the stream in the direction B'ma and I had just come from. He glanced at B'ma, and I realized that the boy was not invited to join us.

We didn't stop when we reached the water but instead continued on a little distance to a place where the rapid flowing stream formed a small deep pool before continuing on at a more relaxed rate. Then I noticed that Uda wasn't carrying a net or spear, only a small gourd, which was slung from his shoulder on a cord. He promptly knelt on the bank, pulled the stopper from the gourd, and poured a portion of the liquid into the pool. Then he smiled with amusement and held the gourd under my nose to smell.

"Holy smokes, Uda. That smells like the drink you used to give me before I went to sleep."

"Juice gives good dreams. Watch now."

Together we sat on the bank. Some fat fish that looked like a type of perch came swimming curiously up when the liquid was poured in. They swam back and forth, more and more slowly, until after a short time they were floating drowsily in front of us. Uda reached down and began to gather them from the water.

"Fish sleeping now, Keeltee. Have good dreams."

Together we hauled out ten or twelve, and then Uda broke off a length of vine from a creeper behind him to string them together.

We sat on the bank of the pool, sunlight and shade dappling the ground, watching the play of the light on the surface of the water. I began to feel as if something momentous was about to take place. It seems very odd, but the atmosphere felt as if it were gathering around us in some way. Uda was enjoying every second. I looked at him; he seemed positively brimming with delight.

"All have agreed, Keeltee."

I was struck dumb. What could he possibly mean? Something was ringing like a distant bell in my head. I shook my head like a prize fighter who's been dealt an unexpected blow. I closed my eyes. I was afraid.

When I opened them again Uda was calmly waiting for me to come to.

"I don't understand," I managed to gasp, afraid to think what he might mean.

"Keeltee, long, longtime ago many groups of S'norra. Plenty women for men. Plenty men for women. It is good." He stopped to see if I understood.

I nodded.

"Longtime ago not many S'norra. For some men no women. Some women no men. Someone has good dream. Dream says good if brothers have one wife, if sisters have one husband. All agree. Is good."

My head was funny again. I shook it, trying to keep my mind clear.

"Okay, I get it. So when the population got too small you agreed that brothers could share a wife and sisters could share a husband."

Uda nodded enthusiastically. I was getting the picture. "Then some time not enough brothers and sisters. Someone has no brother and no wife. Someone has no sister and no husband. No good. Then another good dream. Someone has dream of new ceremony. Can become brother of another. Can become sister of another. First all must agree. Then can become brother, can become sister. Now all have husband. All have wife." He stopped for a moment, then corrected himself. "Almost all have husband. Most have wife."

My mouth was hanging open.

"All have agreed, Keeltee. Anjang agree. Masamo agree. B'ma agree. All S'norra here agree. All hunting party agree. Keeltee can be brother of Masamo. Keeltee can be husband of Anjang."

I gulped. I moved to the water and splashed some in my face. Then I scooped up handfuls and drank them down as if I were dying of thirst, completely forgetting that the water was laced with the green juice. Maybe I got a taste of it and it quieted me down. Finally I was ready to turn back towards Uda.

"You're telling me that I can become a blood brother to Masamo in some kind of ceremony and then I will be married to Anjang. Is that it?"

He nodded.

I was stunned.

"Must get ready, Keeltee. Ceremony tomorrow. Big party." Uda stood and headed briskly back to the compound.

∽ 27 ∽

FORTUNATELY UDA HAD WARNED ME THAT THE NIGHT BEFORE the ceremony I would probably be visited by the ghost beast—and perhaps by the thunder and the lightning beasts as well. Ominous as this sounded, my realization that I was to be with Anjang after all made everything else incidental. I didn't even ask Uda what I should do when the beast approached or how I would recognize it.

Nevertheless I was jolted awake in a sudden panic when I heard the eerie voice calling me. The sound was unlike anything I had ever heard before—deep, low, oboelike, almost cavernous. No human could make a sound like that.

It called me, "Keeltee, Keeltee . . . ," and I have to admit, I was instantly covered with gooseflesh.

At first it seemed to be right next to my head where I lay sleeping on my mat. Then the voice floated out somewhere above me. It was uncanny, elusive. After calling my name a few more times, the ghost beast launched into a beautiful song, poignant and rich with high trills and low sounds like deep growling. Then for a while all was quiet. I went into a kind of peaceful reverie that was suddenly shattered by the sound of a leopard coughing just on the other side of the flimsy leaf wall of my hut.

I leaped off the mat. The beast erupted into a strange profound laughter at my terror. I was glancing around, uncertain about my next move when I heard a completely new sound,

139

but one so familiar, so evocative, that I burst into gales of laughter myself.

Outside my hut, someone was banging on a garbage can lid with a stick.

I'll bet there's no American kid who hasn't done just that on Halloween and probably New Year's Eve as well. It's a sound you can't mistake anywhere. Then I realized what the thunder beast was, and I leaped out the doorway to confront my tormentors.

I caught a glimpse of several men, among them Along and Ete, or maybe Sua, carrying a long pipe of some kind, like an extra long blowpipe, but they disappeared into the gray mist of the early dawn before I could get a clear image of what it was. They were closely followed by several others, one of whom was certainly carrying the suspected garbage can lid. Another bore something else metallic. A long strip of something shiny. They quickly disappeared, leaving me shivering in the damp mist. No way I could go back to sleep now. I went into the hut to collect my bark cloth blanket, then stirred the fire until the banked coals flared up, and sat down, wrapping the blanket around my shoulders, to await the dawn.

To my considerable relief Uda had paid me a prenuptial, or rather, a preadoption, visit the night before. I was beginning to worry about the exact nature of my relationship with Masamo and Anjang. In fact, I had become quite fearful that I would be expected to live with both of them. I'm not particularly religious. I was baptized a Methodist, and my family goes to the Methodist church on an irregular basis. Methodists don't talk much about sex, other than the usual Protestant message—sex is dangerous and dirty so save it for someone you love. Never did quite understand that. I'm not exactly a prude, but I just couldn't imagine a threesome.

Turns out that's not how it works, and thank heavens for that. Uda explained that usually only one of the husbands, or wives, if it's sisters sharing a mate, is home at once. He said Masamo will be leaving after the ceremony with a couple of the others for the "good place" where we camped before. Several different S'norra have dreamed that the Japs are making their way up the bluff. The plan is to keep watch from a safe distance. Uda says not to worry, as we will be gone before they can make it across the chasm. I assume we will move on to another home base somewhere.

In any case, I will have Anjang to myself for quite a while before Masamo returns. Anjang will know when he's coming back, I assume via a dream message, and I will go off to the hunting camp for a bit to give them some privacy. Uda said rather sternly that any expression of jealousy or possessiveness on the part of one of the partners is considered very bad form. I consider myself forewarned. The problem I'm facing, however, is one that can't have come up before.

I want to take Anjang home with me.

I know this deep in my heart. This is not just a convenient temporary alliance for me. This is real.

And since I'm about to become B'ma's father, or one of his fathers, Uda seemed pretty offhand about the nature of our relationship—but hell, I'd like to take B'ma back, too. I love this kid. I'd be a good parent to him, I know. He'd blossom with a good education, and God knows, he's a natural athlete of formidable skill.

I didn't mention these thoughts to Uda, but when the time is right, of course, I'll have to present my case to the entire group. I just hope I know when the time is right.

ONCE AGAIN I WAS PREPARED WITH ELABORATE BODY DECORATIONS, although this time I was painted up like an animal—a gazelle or deer of some kind, I think. Uda wasn't around while I was being adorned, so I couldn't discover the exact significance of the pattern. I did remember that it was similar to the body paint Masamo wore when we arrived, so maybe I'm to look like my adoptive brother. I also have a pretty amazing feather headdress, courtesy of B'ma, and some feather anklets and bracelets to match.

B'ma and a few of the bachelors stayed with me until midafternoon, when everyone left except for B'ma. I was restless and more than a bit nervous, but B'ma wouldn't let me sit down and relax, I guess for fear that I would smear my decorations.

Finally there was some kind of signal, and an hour or two before sunset we began a stately march to the main camp.

There's no doubt about it, the S'norra do love an occasion. Everybody was spiffed up. Uda had on his Davy Crockett hat, and even old Achok had orchid blossoms stuck into the sparse tufts of her hair.

A ritual tent had been constructed, just some bamboo poles stuck into the ground with a roof of leaves, under which Anjang, Masamo, and Uda all sat, smiling like nobody's business, although Anjang held her lovely eyes shyly downcast and didn't meet my gaze. I wasn't sure of the order of business, but B'ma directed me to sit between Uda and Masamo, while he took his place next to Anjang.

We sat politely smiling and nodding while a certain amount of milling around took place. These events always seem to have a spontaneous quality for the S'norra. Takes a while for everyone to get settled and comfortable. It never feels like anything has been rehearsed or planned, more like there's a familiar pattern and then different pieces just occur. Now we had reached the part where everyone waits while looking at everyone else, admiring their ingenious new forms of ornamentation. Indeed, one of the women had fashioned a hat from a small woven basket with a spray of orchids nodding over her brow that could have taken the prize in the Easter parade. It was clear that my feather anklets and armlets were much appreciated also.

Then I heard it again—far in the distance, an almost melancholy, lowing sound, moving through a broad register from a high falsetto to a deep growl. After the ghost beast had sung for a while the garbage can lid was smacked a few times to the delight of everyone. Uda poked me in the ribs and leaned over to say "thunder" with a devilish grin on his face. I heard another sound, no doubt coming from the other piece of metal I had caught a glimpse of that morning. "Lightning," Uda added, smiling with glee.

We all sang for a time, accompanied in a random sort of way by the instruments, which always remained out of sight, either behind the longhouse or in the undergrowth that surrounded the clearing. Then the music died down, and all eyes turned to me.

I looked to Uda for guidance, but to my horror I found he had produced a folding straight-edge razor. He hadn't said anything to me about ritual scarification the night before. Masamo had moved closer to me and put one arm around my shoulders. Before I could speak or protest, Uda quickly gouged three deep notches, one in the center of my forehead and one on each side of my face, just above the cheekbones. I looked into Masamo's face, for the first time noticing the scars that marked him in these exact places, and fainted dead away.

When I came to, Uda was rubbing a kind of ash paste into the cuts, while someone else splashed water on my face to rinse off the blood that was pouring quite freely from the wounds and dripping off my nose and chin. I was feeling pretty shaky. No one seemed the least bit concerned about my momentary faint, and I was helped to sit up again.

Uda asked solicitously, "Can stand now, Keeltee? Time for giving of gifts, yes?" I was worried for a second, as I had heard nothing about gifts and certainly wasn't prepared with any, until Uda brought out the entire stack of blue bark cloths we had created while resting at the good place. I began to struggle to my feet, although I wasn't exactly stable. Masamo moved to stand next to me for support. The tent builders hadn't quite taken my height into account, not to mention my elaborate feather headdress, and to the delight of everyone, when I stood up my entire head thrust through the leaf roof, feathers and all.

Took a while to get sorted out, but finally someone fetched my palm stool from my hut and we got comfortably arranged again, me in the middle, Masamo on my left, carefully dabbing away any blood as it seeped from my wounds. I glanced at Uda again for guidance. "Give one gift and wait, Keeltee," he directed. He didn't say to whom.

I picked up the top cloth and decided to play to the crowd, shaking it out full length on the ground in front of us. Everyone got the cue and oohed and ahhed with appreciation. I stood, carefully avoiding the roof of the tent this time, gathered the fabric up in my arms, and carried it to Va, the lovely young girl a few years older than B'ma, who was seated on some leaves almost directly across from us.

She laughed with delight, nodding at me and smiling joyously as she received the bundle of fabric. Then I returned to my stool and started to reach for another piece of bark cloth, but Uda restrained me with a touch on my arm, nodding towards Va. With the help of several others seated next to her, Va slowly and carefully divided the long piece of cloth into two equal pieces, then rose, first presenting one to a woman I believe is her birth mother and the second of the two pieces to Ete. Her mother and Ete than divided their pieces into two, and these four were presented to others. By this time the pieces were about the right size for a loin cloth. Then Uda gestured to me to present another piece and we went through the entire process again, and so on and on and on. It took quite a while to reach the bottom of the pile, where I had saved the piece of Royal Stewart plaid I'd labored over for last.

I presented it to Anjang, who for the first time that day looked directly into my eyes as she received the gift. I don't know how to describe the look, but it was as if there was no barrier between us. I remembered the first time I had seen her in my dream, when I felt as if I were caught in the force of a great wave. This time I was ready to look back.

When she had divided the cloth, she gave half back to me and half to Masamo. I wasn't sure of the exact etiquette, as I already had another piece, given to me by Along some time earlier in the process, but I was beginning to get into the fun of the ritual. I held up my piece, waved it in front of everyone for their admiration and pleasure, then carefully draped it over Anjang's shoulders. This time she kept it.

While the gift giving was taking place, several large gourds of wine made from the clear liquid drawn from coconuts had been making the rounds, and now pots of food were also circulating among the group. As we ate and drank people would rise to dance around the fire blazing to one side of our circle. I had been helping myself liberally to the drink, probably out of a kind of nervousness—not only was it my adoption ceremony, but according to my own beliefs, I was also facing my wedding night. Finally, I couldn't hold myself back any longer.

I leaped into the center of the circle and threw myself into a wild Highland Fling, kicking my heels out with abandon. I couldn't make a sound like bagpipes, but I managed to burst out with a ringing version of "Scotland the Brave" as an accompaniment. My ecstatic gyrations were met with enthusiastic support, and soon everyone was stamping their feet and clapping along with me.

By now it was completely dark. I had sung and kicked myself through as many verses as I could recall. Quite out of breath, and a bit drunk, I returned to my place feeling very pleased that I had acquitted myself so well with my performance.

Anjang was waiting for me, and with no further ceremony took my hand and led me through the dark night back to my hut, where we would finally be alone.

MY WEDDING NIGHT WAS NOTHING LIKE I HAD EXPECTED. I had convinced Uda that privacy was essential to my marital bliss, and he had extracted a promise from all the bachelors to spend the night in the longhouse, despite their obvious disappointment. Masamo was also in the longhouse; he and three of the others would leave for the good place the following morning.

I thought I would feel shy or ill at ease with Anjang, forgetting the nature of the intimacy already established between us. Our lovemaking was profoundly satisfying, and, at the same time, completely natural. All of the jokes I'd heard and the bad movies I'd seen were ridiculous compared to the reality of our ease with each other.

We spent the entire night making love—and talking. It's funny and I'm embarrassed to admit it, but in some ways the talking was as satisfying as the lovemaking—almost as satisfying, anyway.

To my astonishment Anjang told me about all the times she had seen me—before *Paper Doll* crashed! At first I thought we were having a misunderstanding because of language, but she kept insisting she had seen me frequently and even helped me heal more than once. When I pressed her, she described a time when I was riding on the back of a large brown animal, like a deer but bigger and more friendly. She said I had fallen from the deer and hurt myself here, touching my collarbone as she spoke. She said it was very bad because I had damaged the same place only a short time before. She had seen me hurtling down a mountain very fast, a strange mountain, covered with cold whiteness, and I had fallen again and hurt exactly the same place.

Of course she was right. I broke my collarbone skiing at Hoodoo Bowl the winter I was fifteen, then fell off old Bronc the next spring on my grandfather's ranch and broke it again.

Then she told me about a time I was playing a strange game with other men in which we fought over a large brown coconut and danced together with it. She said I had fallen during the game and hurt my knee badly. Again she visited me, healing me with massage until my knee was well. It took me a minute to get it, and then I fairly split my sides with laughing. That was the time I tore my kneecap playing basketball.

She was full of questions. She wanted to know why boy infants were punished in my country. And did we punish girl infants as well? I had forgotten her reaction to my circumcision. I assured her that circumcision was not a punishment, but she was not convinced. She said "the animals" had a similar ritual, but at least it was done when the boys were older and knew what was happening to them. She said the S'norra believed that "the animals" were so violent because of this foolish practice.

I tried to explain some of the basic facts of hygiene, but she was insulted by what she considered to be my ignorance. She said mothers in my country needed to be taught to wash their boy babies properly, and the boy children taught to wash themselves. This last line was delivered while we were sitting together under the flow of water from the bamboo aqueduct, washing ourselves properly after our third or fourth bout of lovemaking.

She was leaning back against me, half-reclining, while the water splashed on the lovely, soft folds of her vagina. Earlier I had asked her somewhat diffidently if I could look at her more closely—at her vagina was what I meant, of course. She laughed with delight and drew me down between her legs, turning so that the light from the oil lamp fell directly on what I most wanted to see. And see I did.

When we were in San Francisco before we shipped out, Rusty had paid a whore an extra twenty-five dollars to let him look at her. He told me about it afterwards, and I was amazed and pretty impressed by his ingenuity. I would never have thought of such a thing by myself, and yet as soon as I heard about it I knew it was what I wanted to do.

I've seen girlie magazines and I've slept with three women, counting the whore I was with in Frisco, but that's it. Rusty told me that one of his fraternity brothers had warned him never to look at it. The BMOC said if you did, if you actually saw it, you might never get it up again. Rusty told me from that moment on he was trying to think of ways to get a really good look at it. He didn't want to take the chance of dying without having seen the real thing, close up, and in the flesh, regardless of the consequences.

Rusty told me that the whore was quite intrigued by his request and asked him how she looked. He said her vagina was pretty, the lips all ruffled like a party dress. She liked that, I guess. He told me that it was also a little frightening, the structure much more complicated than he had expected.

He assured me it was nothing like the black-and-white line drawings in the sex education manual we'd studied in basic training.

When I first looked closely at Anjang's vagina in the soft light of the oil lamp, I was reminded of one of the black orchids. Her apricot skin darkened to a rich deep mahogany shade between her legs. Her hair there was darker also, very fine and soft, making beautiful symmetrical patterns like watermarks on her thighs and on the pubic mound. Then I thought it was like a pansy—the skin of her inner lips was almost purple, with a softness like petals or velvet.

She showed me a place at the top of the opening. It's quite amazing. There's a little sheath, purplish gray, which can be pulled back to reveal a small, deep pink shaft. I was quite astonished. That's the most sensitive place, like the spot on the underside of my penis, she says. I'm fascinated and startled. I feel like some kind of ignoramus. How come none of us are told about that, I thought? It seems like it's important.

She is charmed by my curiosity and asks me if women in my country are so different. Now that's a hard one. I have to tell her that I don't really know, that in general we don't make a practice of looking there. Then she asks about when we're children, don't we look at one another? She says the S'norran children are always very interested in looking at one another.

I guess I'm a little bit shocked at first. She seems so matter-of-fact about it. And then I remember the summer before the fourth grade. My friend Doug Vincent and I spent a lot of time up in Patty Phetteplace's attic looking at her vagina. Sometimes Judy Hayden joined us. Maybe we showed them our penises, too, but I don't actually remember for sure. I know we never talked about it afterwards, or ever, even though we were all in school together until high school graduation. We sure didn't say anything to anyone else, especially our parents. I guess I was ashamed about it. Probably Doug was, too.

Anjang thinks it is very odd, to be ashamed like that. We've now made love about nine or ten times, and I'm getting a little sore, so she suggests that it might help if she took my penis in her mouth. I won't argue there. She also has a wonderful thing she does just a little after I come. She slips her hand down between us and squeezes the base of my penis, right at the root. I don't know how it works, but I come again and so does she—and it is languorous and slower this time and seems to go on and on and on.

"Keeltee?" Her voice is like brown velvet, like purple pansies. I groan in response.

"When I am little girl I see you, first time." Now I raise myself, resting on my elbow, so that I can touch her face and hair while she speaks. "I am dreaming, yes? But dream is happening somewhere else, not home, not a bad place, but somewhere else."

"Umm hmmm," I murmur drowsily, leaning my face down to take a deep breath of the sweet fragrance of her.

"In this place I am walking along a tree. Tree is great, but down, down on ground, yes?" She gestures, indicating that the tree is fallen. "I am walking along trunk of tree, all alone, looking, looking. Most important for something I am looking." I translated that to mean the thing she was seeking was important to her. "Then I move branch, move leaf like this"—she makes a gesture as if she were holding the branch aside. "You are there, tall boy. You say, 'I have been

153

here all the time, Anjang.' And now I am happy, very glad. It is good." She nods. "Keeltee, most strange you are wearing something white on head, big like this. And shoes on feet like now, but with carving, and animal skins over legs."

Now I am completely awake. "White hat, carved shoes, animal skins" . . . I remember my lifetime dream.

◈ 30 ◈

THE BACHELORS WERE GATHERED AROUND THE FIRE WAITING when we appeared in the morning. I expected sniggers at the very least, but everyone was quite polite. Anjang walked in front of me with an exaggerated stiffness, which I later learned was a conventional way of declaring your partner's sexual prowess. She had told me that all the other women were eager to hear about our night together and she was going back to the longhouse dream circle, leaving me to face the bachelors alone.

I could hardly wait until Uda and B'ma finally turned up. The dream I remembered seemed so important. As soon as we were all seated, I burst out with it.

"Uda! I remembered. Last night I remembered my child-hood dream—at least I think that's what it was."

Everyone else seemed a little disappointed when Uda translated for them. No doubt they were expecting some fascinating revelations about my night with Anjang. Uda, however, was genuinely pleased.

"Anjang told me a dream she had when she was a little girl. Said it was the first time she saw me. I was wearing a white hat, carved shoes, and skins on my legs," Uda obligingly translated. When he said "Anjang" everyone's ears perked up again.

"Then I remembered. I had the dream when I was really little, maybe seven years old. I am in a dance hall, a frontier saloon." Uda had trouble understanding "saloon," but I managed to relate it to the USO club I'd taken my men to, adding that the dream was set in the "longtime ago" world so familiar to S'norran dream lore.

"I'm up on a balcony, looking down at everybody below. I'm a little boy, and I'm dressed up like a cowboy. I have on a big white Stetson, boots, and chaps—I'm wearing chaps. That's what Anjang saw in her dream of me. That's what triggered the memory!"

Now I had to go into a long aside in which I explained something about the romance of the Old West, especially for little boys growing up in Oregon. I tried to explain why cowboys were heroes, especially if they were wearing white hats, and how cowboy boots made you taller, and what made chaps so irresistible a fashion. "Puts your balls in parentheses," was my grandpa's vivid phrase, but I didn't waste time trying to communicate that piece of information.

"Then I see the bad guys below," I said. "They're like the animals and the Japs." Everyone could follow that. "And they've got a whole group of Indians, women and children, too, and the Indians are all tied up, and the bad guys are planning to do something terrible to them." I solved the problem of explaining Indians by describing them as hunters, like the S'norra, who had been overrun by the bad guys and driven from their homelands. Now I had everyone's undivided attention.

"I lasso the big chandelier that looks like a wagon wheel and swing down, smashing into the bad guys and knocking them out. Then I tie them up with my rope and save the Indians."

God only knows what Uda did with "lasso" and "chandelier," but somehow the point got across because when he delivered the last line everyone clapped and stamped their feet.

I also didn't mention that standing among the Indians was a little girl about my own age with long waving hair like dark honey and skin the color of apricots.

"So, what does it mean, Uda?"

He gave me a steady look, oddly hypnotic, compelling. "Little boy knows, Keeltee. Destiny to be hero."

B'ma, however, pointed out that even as a little boy I failed to extract a gift from the "bad guys" once I had vanquished them. General discussion ensued in regard to this recurring oversight. The S'norra suspect that my failure reflected some deep weakness on the part of "my people," and there was much speculation about what happens when you fail to accept the gifts that you deserve, that, indeed, you have earned through your bravery and perseverance. To tell the truth, I am beginning to wonder about it myself. About my whole country, not just myself.

I asked if there was something I could do now to redress this failure. Was it too late for me to collect my gifts? Everyone was very interested in this question. Uda thought it might be important and that the problem should be presented to the entire group for discussion as he has no memory of it ever coming up before.

We wasted no time and immediately joined the larger dream circle from the longhouse. Food was brought out for everyone to share and I am happy to say that Anjang now believes feeding me is her personal responsibility. No pot passed by without being sampled by me. I may actually get enough to eat for once.

Uda delivered quite a long speech in which I assume he explained my problem. Anjang translated a phrase or two for me, but she was more interested in keeping an eye on my nourishment. I didn't want to discourage her, and I was quite sure Uda was doing justice to my dream.

After Uda finished Buteh spoke for a bit. Anjang told me that he was comparing someone who doesn't receive his gifts to a man who plants a crop, tends it, but doesn't harvest the fruit. Buteh sat down, and another hunter spoke. He said someone who doesn't receive his gifts is like a man who travels a long, longway to marry a desirable woman and then doesn't laugh with her. There was general merriment and many sidelong glances at me. Anjang has been moving as if she is very stiff so everyone must know we have laughed many times; however, it was still considered to be a good joke.

As the laughter died down, Achok drew her bent old body upright and pointed two fingers at Buteh with indignation, saying that any fool knew what he and the other hunter had been saying and why were they wasting everyone's time pointing out the obvious. As Achok rose painfully to her feet, everyone else became very quiet. She pointed her two skinny fingers at me accusingly, and I cringed back as she yelled something incomprehensible in my face and then limped back to her place and sat.

Anjang told me that Achok had said I was a poor, ignorant man who needed their help, not their scorn. I was relieved by this, as I thought she might be calling on the others to expel me from the group for my dream failure.

B'ma stepped into the center of the group. First looking at me with his great shining eyes, he then spoke with quiet dignity as he regarded each person in the circle in turn. He said that the S'norra cannot know why my people do not receive their gifts; however, he reminded them that I am the messenger, and I am here to learn from the wisdom of the S'norra. I must do what every S'norran child is taught to do from an early age. I must go back into my dream—he wasn't sure, but he thinks I should go back into both dreams, the beast dream and the cowboy dream—and this time remember to demand my gift. He said that he for one will be there to help me again if called on.

Everyone nodded in agreement, and without further ado the circle broke up and we went about our daily business.

❧ 31 ❧

THE NEXT FEW WEEKS WERE THE MOST BLISSFUL OF MY LIFE. Anjang and I spent most of every day and all of every night together. Our lovemaking became like breathing, as natural and almost as constant. Sometimes we would fall asleep while I was deep inside of her, and we would continue making love in our dreams.

Our most profound lovemaking, however, was not physical. I would lie beside her, gaze into her eyes, and feel myself enter her soul. After a time we would be somewhere else together, some place where even the air was redolent with good feeling. Afterwards I could never remember exactly where we had gone, or what had happened there, but I was sure it was the place the S'norra called home and that we had been there together.

Sometimes I would wake up to find Anjang already gone, a few flowers scattered on the mat next to me. She would rise at dawn, going with one or two of the other women to gather the long green vines with fragrant leaves so favored by the S'norra for necklaces or to drape across doorways, scenting the huts and the longhouse with their balmy sweetness.

When I remembered, I would try to reenter my two dreams as I went to sleep. Some nights I would recreate the cowboy dream, other nights the beast dream. Anjang suggested that I close my eyes and tell her what I was seeing as

I remembered the dream. The details became ever more distinct and rich. I was enjoying the exercise, but I still didn't get any further with the dreams while I was sleeping. It occurred to me that I might ask Uda to give me some of the green juice that had helped me so much at the beginning.

One morning when I woke up to find Anjang already gone, I set out to look for Uda. I knew he made a practice of spending time by the deep pool where he and I had gathered the fish for my adoption feast, so I headed in that direction, grabbing a few roasted tubers from a basket by the door of the hut to munch on as I walked.

I could see him as I neared the pool, sitting upright, unmoving, eyes open. I called out to him, even though I knew he would have heard me approaching. Although my ability to move quietly through the jungle was improving, my arrival was never a surprise to any S'norra.

"Uda!" There was no answer, no movement in response. I came closer. Surely he must have heard me, but he didn't turn his head or even blink his eyes. I stepped next to him, afraid that something might be wrong, and knelt by his side.

"Uda?" This time I was whispering. Still no response. I touched his hand, resting palm up on his thigh. It was very cool, but not cold. Then I did the foolish thing of waving my hand in front of his eyes, and, finally, I placed my hand flat on his chest to see if I could detect a heartbeat. As I did, his eyes flickered for just a second and he slowly raised one hand.

"One moment, Keeltee." His voice was very soft and seemed to come from a long distance away. I lowered my hand, feeling foolish for my concern, and moved back from him a few feet.

"I'm sorry, Uda. I didn't mean to disturb you. I thought something was wrong."

He turned to look at me, and I felt almost dizzy when I met his eyes. Behind him the trees and the foliage blurred for a second though his face stayed in sharp focus, and I wondered if I was about to pass out. Then he lowered his eyelids, and the feeling stopped. He laid one small hand on my arm.

"Soon I will go home, Keeltee. Almost time."

I was shocked, frightened even. Without thinking, I began to protest. "What are you saying, Uda? You can't mean that. You're not sick. Nothing's wrong with you, is it? Tell me what's wrong? Is there some pain somewhere?"

He restrained me with a wave of his hand. "Don't have to kill the body to die, Keeltee. Soon I go home." He spoke with the voice of deep authority that prevented me from protesting further. I looked at the calm surface of the water, trying to make sense of what he said. I could think of no sensible reply to his simple statement. While I was struggling to assemble my thoughts, Uda rose and extended his hand. "Come. I am hungry as wild beast. Let us go eat."

I forgot completely to ask him about the green juice.

The next night, the nightmare began. At first I thought it might have been triggered by my strange experience with Uda, when I thought he was sick or even dead. Although we continued to live in my hut, Anjang usually returned to the longhouse dream circle in the morning, while I made my morning dream reports in the bachelors' circle. When I told my dream, I asked Uda if it might have been caused by my fear of his death. He was thoughtful, closing his eyes for a few moments, before he opened them and replied.

"No, Keeltee, not that. But something. What are you doing last night?"

I replied that I was continuing the work of trying to re-enter my two dreams, and that the night before I had been concentrating on the cowboy dream, telling it in detail to Anjang as I went to sleep, with the intention of demanding my gift from the bad guys. I said that so far I'd had no luck in successfully reentering either dream.

Uda closed his eyes again, then opened them, and suggested I do a test. He said to work with the cowboy dream for one night, the next night the beast dream, the third night neither of the two. He also recommended that I record the nightmare and any further versions of it in my journal. Everyone else thought this was a good idea, and I agreed to the plan.

⟨֍⟩

January 3, 1945 (unsure of exact date, although I believe it's over two months since my last entry—Happy New Year 1945!)

Last night I recounted the cowboy dream from my childhood. Had the nightmare again with a few differences. The first time, night before last, it began with a sky full of mushrooms. They were beautiful, like the fluffy pink and gray mushrooms we frequently gather and eat. I am reminded a bit of umbrellas also, although in my dream the forms had a cloudy shape, not sharp edges. I am looking at them silhouetted against the blue sky. Next I am somewhere, walking, I think. The landscape is gray, desolate, although I seem to be on a path or sidewalk. I am aware of terrible suffering, as if I can hear moans, not screams, but a deep wrenching moan. In fact, I hear nothing. The moaning is somehow inside of me, but I'm not the source of it.

Last night I did the beast dream as I went to sleep. My nightmare started exactly the same way—a beautiful blue sky full of mushrooms, and again I am struck by the beauty of it. In fact, it is more a feeling of awe. I am feeling something like "What hath God wrought?" as I look up into the sky. Then the mushrooms kind of coalesce, until there is just one big mushroom, but it's even more beautiful, and I am looking up at it with a feeling of wonder.

The next thing I remember is the scene of desolation. I can't see clearly. The surreal clarity of the mushroom part is replaced by a thickness. The air is dense, opaque. Everything is gray. Not burned or burning. I don't see any fire, no color, just gray dryness. Wasteland, I think. This time I hear mourning. All inside me. There is no sound outside. No wind. Not a blade of grass or a touch of color. Just gray desolation. I wake up in horror.

Third night I didn't work on either dream, and I didn't have the nightmare. Uda says this is important and he asks me to alternate nights again. He says to do one of the dreams one night, nothing the second, back and forth.

January 12, 1945

I've been alternating nights for nine days now. When I work with either dream, with the intention of demanding a gift from the enemy I have vanquished, I have the mushroom-desolation dream. When I don't, I don't have the dream. Uda asked me to draw the images on the ground. I decided to draw them here in my journal also. The dream has a few variations. Sometimes I can see forms on the ground, like shadows of people. I am reminded of the images of victims from the volcano at Pompcii—always found them to be so moving and evocative. There is no volcano anywhere in my dream, though. I've asked Uda if there is a volcano anywhere near here, and he says not.

I have presented my dream to the entire dream circle twice now. No one seems to understand what it means or how to change it. There have been recommendations to bring water to the landscape. It is so dry and desolate, but I feel helpless when I am there.

I finally remembered to ask Uda about using the green juice again. He said it was a way to get somewhere and that I had needed it at the beginning, but that it would prevent me from learning the route on my own if I were to use it again. I didn't quite follow this, but I trust his judgment about it.

❧ 32 ❧

IN THE MIDST OF MY JOY SUCH SADNESS.

Uda is dead.

It all happened so fast. One day he was here. There was no indication of anything wrong, other than the one experience I had with him by the pool. Then one morning at the end of the dream circle, he spoke to the group for quite a bit. Everyone began to moan and started grabbing ashes from the fire pit and rubbing them in their hair and on their bodies. I was surprised and looked to Uda for an explanation. He said, "Today I am going home, Keeltee." He stood up and began walking away, towards the stream that runs into the pool. I wanted to get up and run after him, to make him come back, but something stopped me. Instead I reached down like the others and began taking handfuls of ashes to rub into my hair and on my body. After a short while we all rose and went to the circle by the longhouse, where everyone else was doing the same.

I went right to Anjang. She looked terrible. Her hair was matted and filled with sticks, her skin filthy from ashes and dirt where she had rolled on the ground. I held her while she shivered and sobbed, great wrenching, heartbreaking sobs. "Anjang, Anjang, don't cry so," I pleaded. But she looked at me with such terrible grief that I begin to sob with her. We clutched each other and wept great shuddering sobs.

167

After a bit a few stood and began to slowly construct a bamboo tent, like the one we sat under when I was adopted. Someone would pound a bamboo pole into the ground for a minute and then fall to the ground, weeping and rolling in the dirt. Along and Buteh were savagely tearing leaves from one of the small huts next to the longhouse. Someone had pulled a stick from the fire and was beating himself on the shoulders with it, wailing and crying. I found this behavior quite appropriate, oddly enough, and joined a pile of others who were rolling around on the ground together.

Eventually the tent was complete and the roof covered with leaves. The wailing quieted down just a little. Several of the men left, although they made no attempt to clean the ashes and dirt from themselves.

Uda appears. I have not seen him walk up. He is just there. His eyes are open and completely serene, the pupils filling the entire socket. He sits on leaves spread beneath the tent. I throw myself to the ground full length in front of him, pleading. "Please, Uda. Please don't die. Please don't. You haven't told me what the messenger is expected to do. Please tell me. Please don't die."

Others join me, weeping and sobbing, although there is no pleading from anyone but me. Anjang sits down next to me with B'ma by her side. The group forms a loose circle in front of the tent where Uda is sitting. Now I hear the ghost beast far in the distance. The sound is deep and heartbreakingly mournful. Then the beast begins to sing. It is a dirge, beautiful and sad, that I dimly remember from the day so long ago when B'ma announced the death of a child at the main camp.

The group quiets now and begins to sing along with the ghost beast. Then comes the refrain, "Oma, oma, rangey, deerantel oplay." It is just too much for me.

B'ma gets up and moves slightly to one side of the group. His eyes are closed, and he is very still, no longer sobbing. After a bit Anjang moves to sit next to him. She also becomes very still, her eyes closed. Gradually their peace seems to penetrate the entire group. Hours must have passed by now. The shadows are long. Someone stands and goes to stir the remains of the fire and add wood, then returns to the group. We continue to sit for what seems like a long time. Every once in a while the ghost beast will sing again, but the others no longer join in. When I hear the refrain from "Home on the Range" again, I can't restrain myself and begin to sob quietly, although everyone else is now still.

The ghost beast is silent, and the small group of men who had left return. I think it must be close to sundown. B'ma opens his eyes and with a joyful shout proclaims something, then looks to Anjang. She also opens her eyes and gives him a radiant smile, nodding. Then she says the same phrase. Everyone shouts joyfully and begins to stand. Ete helps old Achok to her feet. Anjang rises and comes to me. "Keeltee! Uda is home now. Uda has gone home."

Water is brought, and everyone begins to bathe. I feel deeply disturbed. Uda is still sitting there on the leaves in front of us. I go to him, feeling his hand. I press against the pulse point on the inside of the wrist. It is there, just the slightest flutter, distant and weak.

I run to Anjang, "Uda's not dead, Anjang. I can feel a pulse. His heart is still beating. It's not too late. Help me. He's not dead."

She looks at me for a moment, then speaks, slowly and patiently. "Uda home now, Keeltee. Body still here. Body goes soon. Do not trouble Uda. Let body go now."

I am relentless and persist. "Anjang, he's not dead. What makes you think he's gone home? I can feel his heartbeat."

Anjang draws me down beside her. "Keeltee, B'ma and I go home with Uda, yes? Many are there. Heeta is there. Many others. Big party for Uda. Dancing and singing. Here is Uda! Welcome. Welcome. All happy to welcome Uda home. We watch. Cannot stay. But we watch others welcome Uda home.

"Now come, Keeltee. Wash and eat. Dance and sing. Dance and sing with Uda who has gone home. Please."

The last "please" is offered with a deep look, but I'm not ready to join her and the others. I can't believe that they are going to leave Uda alone as he takes his last breath. I go back to the leaf tent, outside the ring of light from the fire which is now blazing high. I sit by Uda and touch his feet. From time to time someone leaves the fire and dancing to come and gently touch me on the shoulder with sympathy.

I remain with Uda throughout the entire night, and when it is morning his body is completely cold, his pulse still.

~ 33 ~

THE NEXT MORNING I WENT BY MYSELF TO SIT NEAR THE deep pool where I had seen Uda such a short time before. I felt stiff, as if I had strained every muscle in strenuous activity. Weariness rose up inside me like water in a spring. Pain inside and out. I wanted to continue mourning for Uda. I also wanted to think about the day before.

My grandparents died a few days apart from each other during the terrible flu epidemic the winter I was seventeen. I remember the funeral. I remember family and friends standing around our dining room table afterwards, balancing plates piled with sandwiches and coffee cake. The men all wore dark suits. The women had on navy blue or black dresses, except Aunt Gladys, who wore navy with white polka dots. I know my mother found her wanting in respect from the way Mom held her mouth when she looked at Gladys.

Someone had called the school to tell me when Grandma died. The principal asked if I wanted to go home. I said no and finished the day. Grandpa must have died on the following weekend. Dad came home and told me. There was sorrow in our house, weariness too. Mom and Dad must have been spending a lot of time out at the ranch caring for them. I don't remember much outright crying. My sister cried at the funeral, but she was only twelve. There was some kind of unspoken feeling that it was important to bear up in some way. I didn't talk to my friends about the deaths, and no one said anything to me, although I can remember walking down the hall at school the next week, hearing someone behind me tell someone else in a hushed voice that my grandparents had died from the flu.

What else? I loved my grandparents. Why didn't I wear my kilt to the funeral? I should have. My grandmother would have wanted me to. I should have worn my kilt and cried out loud like I did yesterday. And where did my grandparents go? What did they think happened when you die? Why didn't anyone ever talk about that?

I cried some more, but now I wasn't mourning Uda; I was crying because I didn't tell my Grandpa and Grandma how much I loved them before they died. Once the tears got going I could think of all kinds of good reasons to cry. I thought about Rusty Cable paying the prostitute for a look at her vagina and cried about that. I cried about Tom Tully riding the rails to get to a draft board where no one knew him so he could lie about his age in order to enlist and then die when *Paper Doll* crashed. I cried for all of my men. And then I cried for Uda. Why hadn't he told me what I was expected to do before he died?

At last, I cried for myself.

That's how Anjang found me, sitting by the pool with tears running down my face, my shoulders shaking as I sobbed. She didn't say anything. She just sat down next to me, at first quiet. After a bit she began humming something, not a dirge this time, just a low tone that would shift a little bit up and down. She rocked back and forth very slowly while she hummed. Gradually I began to feel better. When my sobbing stopped, she filled her cupped hands with water and rinsed my face, smiling softly but not speaking. She sat down next to me. We sat together for a while, looking at the water.

"Anjang? The place where you go, where you and B'ma saw Uda, that you call home—how do you get there? If I learn to go there, can I find my grandparents who are dead? Can I visit Uda? How can I find out how my men are doing?"

Anjang didn't answer immediately. When she was finally ready to answer, she spoke slowly, thoughtfully. "Keeltee, I think is like a path. I follow this path since I am a little girl. I know the way. It is our way. All S'norra know this path." She looked at me with vast tenderness. "We call you messenger, Keeltee. To deliver message must follow the path."

I shook my head in frustration. "I don't know the way, Anjang! And I don't know what the message *is* either."

She reached up and smoothed my hair away from my face. "Not to worry, Keeltee. You learn quick, quick."

ᵥᵥ 34 ᵥᵥ

AFTER UDA DIED, ANJANG JOINED OUR DREAM CIRCLE EVERY morning. I was getting better at understanding S'norran. I could usually get the gist of most conversations, but I still couldn't speak very well, and I needed help with translation to participate in the circle. One morning B'ma remarked that he had a new idea for me. Everyone was still very interested in my attempts to reenter my dreams and ask for my gifts. B'ma wanted to know if I had any ideas about what form the gifts might take when I finally managed to get them.

I actually hadn't thought much about it. The dream gifts most S'norra receive seem related to their greatest interests; hunters like Ete and Sua wake up with plans in their heads for a new kind of trap or they dream about the best site for hunting that day—they'll even be shown the animal that is waiting for them there. Someone who works in the garden a lot will have a dream about a better way to clear the forest or how to build an aqueduct. What did I want or need? Once I asked that question I knew I was beginning to get somewhere. There were some areas where I really needed help. I remembered Masamo recounting his childhood dream where the spirits taught him to fly. Now I was starting to feel excited. I told B'ma that I thought his idea was a very good one and that I would think carefully about the gifts that I most wanted and needed.

Later that day Masamo and Ete appeared to tell us that "the animals" had been sighted not too far from the good place. Their appearance confirmed a dream one of the hunters had reported a day or so before in the longhouse dream circle, and it was generally agreed that if "the animals" were near then the Japs were not far behind.

Ete returned to the other men who were keeping watch at the good place. Masamo would go to confer with the group at the nearby hunting camp. Without being told, I realized that Anjang would accompany Masamo. I reminded myself that it was only for a few days, and then she would return to me. I was relieved that there were no good-byes and that no one else seemed to take any notice of their departure. I decided I would spend my time in her absence giving serious attention to my dream assignment. Specifically, I would work on identifying the gifts I most needed.

But, of course, dreams have a way of surprising you. As soon as Anjang was absent from my bed a whole new problem turned up. I felt fortunate that in her absence I could avoid reporting my dreams in the circle, even though B'ma asked me every morning. I decided instead that I would continue my dream record in my journal.

⚜

January 27, 1945

Anjang gone for the first time. I'm not having the mushroom-desolation dream, but I almost wish that I were. What's happening is much worse. Last night I had a long and very exciting sex dream with Va, a young girl who is probably twelve or thirteen years old at the most. What makes it even more reprehensible is that in the dream I seem to be aware of the actual circumstances of my life. That is, I remember that I am married to Anjang. I know that Va is a very young girl. And yet I seem to have no compunction at all about engaging in the most intimate acts with her. It's true that in the dream she approaches me, but that's no excuse. I feel like some kind of pervert.

I've also been thinking about the gift I want to receive. I want to learn how to "go home," as the S'norra say, which seems to mean visiting the place where most of their dead friends and relatives are now. I wonder if this is what Methodists call heaven?

B'ma wants me to teach him how to write. He's interested in the marks I make in the journal. I've started teaching him the alphabet, using the children's singing rhyme, which he learned perfectly in about five minutes. We're also working on a map of the whole area together. It's amazing to me how quickly he can grasp concepts that must be completely foreign to him. When I asked him how he could pinpoint different trails and directions so easily (at least that's what I think I asked—we're still struggling with some words) he showed me that he flew over different areas at night while he was dreaming. That's a skill that could have real value in wartime. I think it's also how the hunter who saw "the animals" knew they were at the bluff.

B'ma and I have made a map of the entire area, including the hunters' camp and the trail down the bluff to the site of the crash. We've used a large scale with lots of detail, drawing it out on a piece of bark cloth. I'm going to reduce it and include it here. We've also mapped a secret trail that leads from here to the bottom of the bluff, but on the other side from the crash site. B'ma tells me only S'norra know about this trail, which is very narrow and difficult to follow. I asked him if this is the direction Uda took when he went to the clinic but B'ma doesn't know.

January 29, 1945

Two more nights of dreaming about Va. Last night I finally managed to avoid the actual act, although just barely. In the dream Va was very hurt by my refusal. I have noticed that she is avoiding me during the day, which makes me think that she must somehow know about the dreams. I feel a lot of shame about my behavior and a certain amount of confusion besides. I have decided that I must be completely truthful with Anjang and ask for her advice as soon as she returns. I wish Uda were here. I don't think I can mention these matters to B'ma, although he is letting me know that he is aware something is wrong. I finally told him that I had some bad dreams and that I was writing them down so I could tell them to Anjang. That seemed to reassure him.

⋙ 35 ⋘

I GUESS IT'S SAFE TO SAY THAT I AM COMPLETELY ASTONISHED. When Anjang returned, I wasted no time before telling her about my erotic dreams with Va. Her response was a complete surprise. First she chuckled. Chuckled!

"Anjang, I don't understand what's going on! How can you laugh at this?"

"Keeltee, Va comes to you for teaching. When you are laughing with Va most important you give her good pleasure. Must come, Keeltee. Both come when you are with Va, yes?"

I couldn't reply to this. I sat down very heavily on the ground—we were about halfway to the deep pool where we had established a ritual of swimming and bathing together every afternoon. I put my head in my hands and groaned.

Anjang picked two or three leaves and took her time about fastidiously arranging them next to me before she sat down, looking up at me curiously.

I had a hard time thinking of what to say. "Anjang, Va is just a girl. Where I come from it is very bad to laugh with little girls. Men are punished for doing this, and it's a good thing for them to be punished."

Anjang listened to me and nodded. "Bad if take Va to jungle and laugh with her, yes, but you laugh in dream, Keeltee. Moon has visited Va. Now her time for dream lover, yes? How do you learn to laugh if no dream lover?"

179

I didn't have an answer to that one. All I could do was groan and shake my head. Anjang had an expression on her face that reminded me of the times when Uda was so obviously troubled by my lack of education. Finally, I said, "Could you explain it to me? Va has been avoiding me since it happened. How can it be all right for me to laugh with her in dreams? I don't understand at all."

Anjang nodded sympathetically. "When girl chooses dream lover from group, must stay away from him awake, yes? Otherwise trouble sometime. Bad to look at Va or speak. But time of great happiness, great joy. Girl very happy, oh so pretty, soon will be laughing with someone." Now Anjang stood up in front of me and paraded around with her breasts stuck out provocatively. "She does this . . ."—Anjang curved her back and waved her almost completely naked buttocks in my face—"and this. . . ." She leaned across so that her lovely breasts brushed my face. "Men think, 'Oh, holy cow, maybe Va choose me for dream lover,' especially very old men think this. Is great honor to be dream lover, Keeltee."

I was still numb with shock. I sat, trying to imagine what would have happened if my teenage sister had waved her naked breasts and buttocks in the faces of old men. I had to smile. My sister would have loved it. I made an inner vow to tell her some day what she had missed.

When we got to the pool, we took our time in the water, enjoying the knowledge that eventually we would swim over to the other side, where a screen of tall shampoo plants hid a perfect moss-filled hollow, just the right size for two people. To my surprise I had no thought of Anjang's recent journey with Masamo. It had been easier than I expected to accept that she had two husbands, although I imagine it would have been a different story if I'd been the first of them.

But I still couldn't let go of my concern about Va. Something about it just didn't feel okay to me. I lay next to Anjang, looking into her eyes, enjoying the openness of her look; I knew I could tell her anything. There was nothing false in her. The trick for me was explaining in some clear way what my conflict was.

"Anjang, I need to know more about this dream lover business. Is there a way I could arrange for someone else to take my place? Does everyone have a dream lover? What happens with your dream lover when you marry? It's not something we do where I come from, and I'm having trouble understanding what's going on."

She looked away, thinking my question over, but before she could reply I had remembered something else I needed to confess. "There's one other thing that might be important. The last time we were together I didn't laugh with her, even though she wanted to very much. I thought I was being responsible, but now I'm not so sure."

Anjang frowned, then nodded. "Keeltee, when I am girl like Va I am laughing with Masamo, with some others before moon comes to me, before dream lover. Then dream lover comes and teaches me, but not man of here, man of spirit, yes? Once here, now home. He is showing me much. I learn good ways to laugh, like others. But I learn much else. I learn to not have children. I have B'ma, but no more. B'ma comes when I am small, not tall like now." She was quiet for a moment, frowning a little as she searched for the correct terms in English. "Va different. No husband here for Va. No children. Only dream lover." She raised herself on one elbow so she could look into my face. "Tell Va in dream you most sorry and give fine gift, yes? Good, Keeltee?"

I nodded, even though I was still feeling a little confused. "One last question, Anjang? Do the others know that I am Va's dream lover?"

"Not good form to tell dream lover's name, Keeltee." She smiled. "But not hard to see who Va not speaks to, not looks at."

It didn't occur to me at the time to ask why B'ma wasn't a prospective husband for Va. Of course, he was younger, but that wouldn't be important in a year or two.

Anjang was very impressed with the map B'ma and I had designed, although at first she thought I had reentered one of my dreams to receive the inspiration for it as a gift. When I told her it was a system used in my country for a long, longtime, she then assumed it had been given to one of my ancestors in a dream, and I suppose she may be right.

I asked if she knew which direction Uda had taken when he went in search of the clinic so long ago. She didn't know, but she did point to the secret trail leading down to the bottom of the bluff at its southern side.

"Uda comes back from here. Good trail, Keeltee. Small animal trail. Like this." She mimed leaning over, as if the foliage made a narrow tunnel. "Safe." I would remember her words a few weeks later.

❧ 36 ❧

THE GROUP FROM THE HUNTING CAMP HAS MOVED BACK TO
the main settlement. I think we will all be moving on soon.
Ete has come to inform us that he and the others at the good
place have decamped to our side of the chasm, where they
have built a new camp close to the place where Masamo had
the arrow pulled from his thigh. Ete says that "the animals"
are a constant presence on the other side. Our men pulled
the vine bridge completely over, even pulled away the fine
cord that is usually kept connected to the other side.

Things here go on much as before. There is no sense of
urgency or danger, although I feel that something has changed.
If anything, it's a bit more festive than usual. I suppose we
wait until someone has a compelling dream detailing the
information about where to move.

There is dancing almost every night. It's something to
watch. It starts slowly. Someone gets up and moves around
the fire, stamping his or her feet and clapping to the sound
of the singing. Gradually the speed of the dancing increases,
and others join in until there's a circle moving together. Then
the leaping starts. I've never seen anything quite like it. Ete
and Sua are the best, although there's a woman named Alo
who's pretty good, too. I can never tell how old the S'norra
are, but her curly hair is gray so she must be middle-aged,
although you'd never know it to see her leap.

There's no warm-up. Almost no sinking or knee bending before the leap either. Alo just seems to rise into the air. Each time she jumps there's a wave of clapping and foot stamping from the others. Then Ete and Sua leap, or rise, and it turns into a kind of pattern. I've seen them go straight up with no preliminary windup, just up into the air three or four feet. It gets really exciting. I asked Anjang how it's done. She says the dancing lifts you. You can't just stand up and do it at any time. You dance for a while and then the dancing lifts you.

I get up and perform a Highland Fling now and again when the fancy takes me. Keep hoping that the dancing will lift me, too, but so far not.

I've rescued the remaining two detonators from where they were stored in Uda's cubicle. They're kept well packed in moss in the bottom of my own carrying basket, which is almost twice as big as anyone else's. It's a beautiful thing, woven and decorated for me by Achok. I've been the recipient of many presents since I started working on reentering those two dreams. It's as if everyone has agreed to prime the pump, so to speak. Almost every day someone makes something for me.

I'm also the proud new keeper of the garbage can lid, or thunder beast, which Anjang tells me is quite an honor. It is kept wrapped in bark cloth in the rafters of the longhouse. It's my job to bang it when the ghost beast is on the prowl, which sometimes happens during the evening festivities. The pitch rises to a certain point, and then it's considered appropriate for the beasts to come out. I'm getting much better at knowing just when that moment is reached.

I've also seen the ghost beast. It's a long section of bamboo, hollowed out. Some of the men are real virtuosos on it, making it sob like an infant, or wail like an animal. The women play other instruments, including a small stringed lute and drums, but men handle the three beasts. It's the only area where I've noticed a real difference between men's territory and women's. All other activities are shared more or less equally, except hunting. A couple of the women use bows and arrows, but I haven't seen any woman use a blowpipe.

It's been hard for me to assess the degree of danger we're actually in. I have tried to discuss plans for our defense with Anjang, but she is only mildly interested in my speculation. She'll listen politely for a bit, but soon she moves on to something else. Nevertheless, I am making plans. If the Japs bridge the chasm, I know I can take the bridge out with the detonators. I'd have to use them both. I worried for a bit that using them might reveal my presence, which could lead to terrible retribution on the S'norra if any were captured. The Japs have been vicious to local tribes who collaborated with the Allies or who concealed downed pilots. I felt it was necessary to discuss the matter with the group as a whole, but Anjang has assured me that it will not be a problem.

I couldn't let it go at that, and I described to her what the Japs were capable of. She agrees with Uda that they're insane, but still feels certain no one will be captured by them. It's funny. There seems to be no word in S'norran for evil. Enemies are considered to be ignorant. In fact, most wrongdoing is seen as the product of ignorance, and I guess I'd have to agree with that.

I've talked to Anjang more about the whole dream lover business. I did meet with Va again, in dreams, of course, where I apologized and presented her with a nice corsage. Seemed like the thing to do. Anjang says that most S'norra start having visits from a dream lover just before puberty. Sometimes it's actually a family member, a parent or brother or sister. She says it's not done to laugh with your parents or siblings, of course, but that spirits often come in the guise of family members at first as they are already known and loved by the young person. I asked if it was likely that a spirit might take my place with Va. I'm feeling a little less uncomfortable with the whole thing, but I'm still nervous; it goes against all of my upbringing.

I tried to imagine what it would have been like when I was a teen if a beautiful woman started meeting me in my dreams for the sole purpose of training me in the arts of love. Then I tried to imagine my parents encouraging me to give my dream visitor pleasure and especially to bring her to orgasm. Needless to say, I find it inconceivable. My dad talked to me about sex once or twice, but the conversation was clinical and pretty basic. He said it would be better if I saved myself for the woman I loved, but if I didn't to be sure to wear a condom. Pleasure and the importance of bringing your partner to orgasm didn't enter into it.

Anjang says that laughing with someone is extremely important because when it's done very well you remember what it is like to be home. I guess this means that to the S'norra sex is heavenly. I'm beginning to think they're right about that.

I guess I would rather make love to Va at night than have the mushroom-desolation dream. Seems like it's one or the other every night. The mushroom dream seems endless when I'm in it. The desolation is so unimaginably vast, and it goes on and on while I'm trudging endlessly through it. It's such a relief when I wake up and find myself in this green, fragrant paradise with Anjang by my side. It's like the difference between heaven and hell. I'm beginning to think it's a dream about hell. Hell isn't burning and hot like the Bible says; it's a place of exhaustion and gray desolation that goes on eternally.

SOMETHING IS UP. I CAN FEEL IT. IT'S LIKE THE TIME JUST
before the big event, graduation or something. A time of antici-
pation and excitement. Like Christmas is coming or some important holiday. Masamo, Ete, and the others have returned
from the new camp on this side of the chasm. Anjang spends
some nights with Masamo in the longhouse, but most nights
with me. Masamo is usually gone every day, hunting and foraging. Sometimes she goes with him, but more often stays around
the camp and we take long leisurely walks and swims together.

Masamo has made me a beautiful bow, wonderfully carved
and inlaid with pieces of bone, then polished until it shines. I
am quite touched by the gift and tell him so. I feel bad that
I don't have any skills that measure up to the S'norran talents.
Anjang says it's not necessary to gift the giver; that my presence is a gift to them all. She tells me this with such complete
sincerity. I feel overwhelmed, but also unworthy of such regard.
I'm not special in any particular way that I know of. I'm reasonably honest, certainly capable. I believe I was a responsible
leader of my men. Damn, I wish I knew what I'm expected to
do. Whatever it is it can't be far away. Something is impend-
ing. I feel it when I wake up every morning.

The celebrating continues every night. It's not considered
polite to leave until the dancing is over, although it is acceptable
to take short naps while it's going on. Regardless of how late

things continue, we still hold our morning dream circles, even if a lot of us go back to sleep after. Feasting, dancing, and sleeping seem to be the way we're preparing for the big move ahead.

I have learned that a large group of men and piles of supplies have been assembled on the far side of the chasm. I've tried without success to organize a party to reconnoiter. It's frustrating, to say the least. If the Japs are getting ready to bridge the chasm, I need to know about it. Everyone here is so unconcerned. I will think that two or three of the men have agreed to go, but the next morning the plan melts away; someone wants to hunt, others are too tired from the dancing and want to sleep. It's as if no one is at all interested in the Japs or what they are doing. I've talked to Anjang about it, and about my belief we need to be well away from here. She tells me with complete confidence that we are not in danger.

She has made me a very handy first aid kit, including some leaf packets like the ones Uda carried filled with antidotes to various poisons and snakebite, herbs for fever, and a stoppered gourd filled with the very same healing gel that she massaged me with in those dream visits. She says it's good for all kinds of things from charley horse to serious burns or infection. She's also laying in a store of prepared food like we ate on that first trek, which is reassuring. At least we'll have some supplies if we need to pull out in a hurry. I've become quite good at sniffing out edible roots and tubers. For a while I played a kind of game with B'ma, who would assemble a collection of various kinds of roots, mushrooms, and berries; then I would identify which ones were good and which were inedible or poisonous. It's interesting to me that the good ones often grow very close to the most dangerous roots, with leaves that are strikingly similar.

190

⮞ 38 ⮜

LAST NIGHT SEVERAL OF US HAD DREAM VISITS FROM UDA! In my dream I found him sitting by the deep pool, just as he was the day I saw him and thought something was wrong. I was so happy to see him—it was like a shaft of joy shot through me. Then I remembered he was dead and stopped in my tracks. I heard his funny, tinkling laugh, and he turned his head and looked at me.

"Uda! I can't believe you're really here. There's so much I want to talk to you about."

"Why worried, Keeltee?"

"The Japs are coming. They're at the chasm. I think they're going to build a bridge across. I can take the bridge out with the detonators. Is that what I'm supposed to do? But no one else seems very worried. Shouldn't we be moving? Are you here to tell me what to do?"

"Almost time now, Keeltee. In only a few days all finished. Not to worry. No problem now."

Then I remembered. I hesitated for a moment. Of course, it was what I needed to do. I'd been struggling for weeks to remember. I threw myself on the ground in front of Uda. The bank sloped down to the water at a slight angle so that as I sat before him my head was slightly lower than his. I looked up at him. "Uda?"

His face broke into that familiar, endearing network of delicate folds and wrinkles as he smiled broadly. He nodded.

191

"Please give me a gift."

He laughed outright. "Very good, Keeltee. You learn quick, quick." He reached forward and laid his small hand on the crown of my head as he spoke. "Time is close. Messenger is ready. When time comes you will know what to do." My eyes closed, and I inhaled deeply. I felt something like warmth or light entering my mind. Soft and very comforting, it gently melted my worries away. For the first time, I felt I could relax.

The entire group met at the longhouse fire for the dream circle. More than half of us had received visits from Uda. I reported first. Everyone was pleased to hear that I had finally remembered to ask for my gift.

All the other visits were different. One woman heard Uda's voice speaking to her. Buteh thought he woke up to find Uda standing at the foot of his sleeping mat. But the messages were all the same. Uda encouraged each of us, telling us that things were in order and the time was near. I have concluded I don't have to keep going back to my old dreams. I've finally done what I needed to.

I had expected that the feasting and dancing that night would reach a kind of fever pitch, but instead it was gentle, almost dreamlike. The most extraordinary thing was the leaping. Ete started it. Almost everyone was dancing, but at a slower, more meditative pace than usual. When Ete leaped the first time, I couldn't quite believe what I'd seen. It was as if he lifted into the air and then floated for a second. Then others were doing it. Rising into the air, floating in space, and gently settling back down. Anjang was next to me, quietly rocking Katala, the toddler, who was sleeping peacefully in her arms. I looked over at her, but she only nodded, as if to reassure me that I had seen what I had seen. I wanted very much to get up and join the dancers, to rise and float like that, but something held me back. It was almost as if they were suspended in water, rising, heads raised, floating in space for a moment, and then slowly, softly, settling back down to the ground.

A short time later Anjang handed the toddler to one of the other women and held out her hand to me. I wondered if it was all right for us to leave the group still dancing and floating, but like the laws of gravity the usual rules seemed to be suspended. The night was magical. Light from an almost-full moon covered everything with a silvery glow so that even small pebbles were sharply defined by it. Mist hung in the tops of trees, drifting down to rest where the ground was low. I was feeling some concern that Anjang had not been visited by Uda, but when I asked her she only laughed and reminded me that she and B'ma were waking dreamers. She said Uda was close to her almost all the time. I looked at her face in the moonlight, and it seemed to me that she was like a spirit herself. It must have been a trick of the light, but it was almost as if she flickered in and out in front of me. I grasped her arm, reassuring myself that she was still solid, present, with me.

We made love in the silvery light, where the moon's path shone through the doorway of the hut and across the sleeping mat. I seemed to melt into her. We hardly moved. I looked into her eyes and held her. She started to come before me, and I felt myself being drawn into her. It was like being pulled deeper and deeper inside, until I began to reach orgasm myself. Then it was as if I lost consciousness temporarily. I didn't, couldn't, resist the feeling of being drawn out of myself. I was falling, or floating—it made no difference at all. Then it was dark.

I don't know if time passed, but it seemed after a while that Anjang and I were flying together. Images became very crisp, not floating and misty, but sharp and clear. I could feel the air growing increasingly cool and thin as we rose above the earth. Below me were patterns of light and darkness, plus a few twinkling spots of illumination. It was completely familiar. After all, I had flown above this territory for months in *Paper Doll*. I held Anjang's hand, and she seemed to lead me. Our progress was effortless, even though my body had mass and weight. We gripped our hands together tightly. I could feel the strength of her grasp. She raised her other hand and pointed at a spot in the middle of the brilliant mass of stars filling the sky like a cascade of silver light.

We continued to move in the direction that she had indicated, but now I seemed to be floating in light, surrounded by the exquisite silver light, effervescent, touching me, exploding against my skin with a sensation that sent shivers of joy and delight coursing through me.

The next thing I knew, Anjang and I were standing at the foot of a staircase leading up to a longhouse, but a longhouse unlike any I had ever seen or imagined. Anjang started up the stair in front of me, glancing back over her shoulder to make sure I was following her. I hung back for just a moment, gazing up at the structure which seemed so beautiful, so perfect to me that I wanted to memorize each detail. I thought, *Yes, this is how it ought to be. This is what I imagined it was like.* Some deep feeling inside of me seemed confirmed by the existence of this majestic structure.

Inside it was even better. The space was vast, but intimate. Lights glittered from the walls and from a magnificent chandelier, shaped like a huge wagon wheel, suspended in the center of the hall.

As we stepped through the door, B'ma ran to Anjang, throwing his arms around her knees. All the others gathered around us, welcoming us, greeting us with garlands of flowers and strands of the fragrant vines so loved by the S'norra. Everyone was there. Heeta lifted me off the ground with his hug. Old Achok brought me a necklace of flowers. She seemed youthful, moving with grace and ease, not the usual stiffness and pain that I remembered. Ahead I could see younger, fit-looking Ada and Ata sitting together on a raised dais—with Uda next to them! He gave a merry wave and nodded to me.

It was all so beautiful. I felt like I couldn't contain the feelings of joy that kept moving through me in great bliss-filled waves. Then I looked up. Around three sides of the space was a balcony, with an interior staircase on my right. Leaning over the balcony and waving down to me were my grandparents! I had to chuckle when I saw them. My grandpa was dressed in one of his old striped flannel nightshirts, and my grandmother wore a favorite light blue dressing gown. They were so delighted to see me. "Tell everyone we said hello," my grandfather yelled down at me, and I nodded back vigorously.

Anjang took my arm and drew me towards the far left of the vast space which seemed to expand in several directions. In front of us was an arched doorway with a sign above it reading "Victory Bar." I looked inside. Round tables filled the space; the air was blue with smoke from fat cigars. They were all there. The entire crew from *Paper Doll* sat together, whiskey bottles on the tables, jackets slung over the backs of their chairs, hats tipped back on their heads, playing poker! Tom Tully looked up to see me. "It's Kilty! Kilty's finally made it! Come on in, Captain, and take a hand. Rusty, pour out a drink for Kilty. He's here!"

I started to step in, but Anjang drew me back with a smile, shaking her head. I waved instead and called out. "Good luck with your game, guys. Take it easy. I'll see you later, okay?"

I looked down at her, gathering her close to me with my arm around her shoulders. "This is really great. I knew it would be like this."

She didn't answer, but raised on her toes, placing her hands on either side of my face, and drew me down closer to her. She gazed into my eyes for a long time with a look of the deepest love, then kissed me gently, and led me back to the doorway, where she stood, watching and waving, as I descended the long staircase.

I woke up. It was very early, just light. I rolled over to Anjang, but she was already up and about. I wanted to tell her my dream. I lay back for a moment and closed my eyes. I wanted to make sure each detail was firmly cemented in memory. It was far too precious to lose even a single image or feeling. I felt deliciously safe and warm, as if nothing would ever trouble me again. I smiled, remembering my crew puffing away on those big stogies. I had even seen the ice in the highball glasses. Did that mean there was whiskey in heaven? I couldn't wait to tell Anjang about it and find out. Was that real? Was that what it was really like?

I pulled myself to my feet and went out to the aqueduct to splash water on my face. I kept a piece of soft stick with a frayed end in a bamboo cup next to the water pipe to use as a primitive toothbrush. While I was brushing I looked around. The mist was still rising from the ground as the sun began to warm it. What a night it had been.

I stirred the fire and tossed a few pieces of wood on. None of the bachelors seemed to be up yet. Where was everybody? God only knew how long the dancing and leaping had gone on the night before. Maybe everyone was still sleeping. I went back to the hut and searched around until I found a couple of sweet potato–like tubers to munch on.

It was going to be a beautiful day. A coolish breeze stirred the huge fronds of the coconut palms above. I grabbed the end of one that had come down during the night and pulled it to the edge of the clearing out of the way, then I wandered over to the main fire where we had feasted the night before. To my surprise the fire was completely out. I picked up a long stick and stirred it for a moment. That was very odd. It was quite unlike the S'norra to allow a fire to die like that. "Anjang?" I called out, glancing around me with just a touch of unease. It was very odd that no one was about. I'd heard nothing about a hunting expedition the night before, and even if there were one, someone always stayed behind. Besides, there hadn't been a dream circle yet. I smiled to myself, remembering. I wanted to report every detail, to check what I had seen and felt with the others who had all been there, too.

I looked up at the longhouse, comparing it in my mind with the magnificent structure I had seen the night before. Was it Plato who said that perfect versions of everything in the world existed somewhere? I had never quite understood what he was talking about, but the longhouse in my dream was certainly a perfect version of something.

I walked over to the longhouse. It had no windows. The loosely woven walls allowed sufficient air to circulate without them, and kept it cool inside during the day. I didn't often go inside, anyway, respecting the space that Anjang and Masamo occupied together, but maybe someone was there this morning. I went to the ladder and looked up at the doorway, but couldn't see into the dark interior. "Anjang?" I called again. "B'ma?" No one replied. I called out a greeting word in S'norran and waited. Still no answer.

Wouldn't hurt to go inside, I thought. But something stopped me. It wasn't exactly a feeling of dread. Something else. I climbed the ladder cautiously, listening to hear if anyone was moving around inside.

When I stepped through the door, I couldn't see much at first. The day was bright now, and the interior was dim. It took a moment for my eyes to adjust, and when I could see better I had to smile. The entire space was draped in the garlands of flowers and long chains of fragrant leaves that everyone had been wearing in my dream the night before.

I went to the opening of the first cubicle and glanced inside. Along and his wife were lying asleep on their mats with Katala curled between them. I didn't want to wake them, so I moved on to the next cubicle, where I found Achok sleeping away. Then to the next, where a couple from the hunter's camp were asleep. Directly across from this cubicle was the space where Anjang and Masamo slept. I looked inside. They lay next to one another on their mats. Anjang wore white orchids in her hair. B'ma was next to her. I went in and laid my hand on Anjang's cheek. She was completely cold to my touch, as were Masamo and B'ma.

I went to each cubicle now, touching each person very carefully. Finally, I climbed up to the dais at the end, where Ata and Ada lay together. They, too, were cold. Everyone was cold. Everyone was dead. Completely, absolutely, dead forever.

FOR QUITE A WHILE I SAT IN THE MIDDLE OF THE LONGHOUSE, rocking back and forth and humming to myself. Then I got up and went from space to space again, checking on everyone one more time. How could B'ma and Katala be dead? This time I looked for evidence of the cause of death. A gourd holding poison seemed likely. I remembered that in my high school production of *Romeo and Juliet,* Juliet had tried to drain a few drops of poison from the bottle in order to join her lover. I knew I was being foolish. The knowledge of my foolishness didn't stop me from searching. I found Uda's straight-edge razor, the one used during my adoption ceremony. Maybe I even had a thought of using it. But my friends had not killed themselves.

I went to the fire and rolled around in the ashes for some time. I wasn't crying, but I did let out a couple of strange, strangled cries. After a while I fell asleep, lying there covered with ash and filth from the fire.

When I woke up, it was afternoon. I went to the aqueduct and washed myself thoroughly. Then I entered our hut and carefully packed everything I would need, after first removing the detonators from my carrying basket. Anjang had made sure that all I would require for my journey was ready. I wrapped a few glowing coals from the bachelors' fire in green leaves to place in the top of the basket, as I had seen the others do so many times before.

I went back to the longhouse and climbed the ladder. The flowers and leaves smelled wonderfully. I checked everyone again, but no miracle had brought them back to life. I kissed Anjang and B'ma. The last thing I did was to take down the thunder beast from the rafters. When I was outside, I unwrapped it and tied it by the handle to the back of my carrying basket.

Then I piled some dry tinder at either end of the longhouse. I placed each detonator where the fire would set it off within a half an hour or so. I unwrapped my coals and used them to ignite the tinder. In only a few minutes the fire had flamed up and caught the dry mats that formed the walls of the longhouse.

I started down the trail that led to the hunters' camp. I knew the secret trail cut off to my right after a walk of an hour or so. Before I reached it an enormous explosion shook the ground underneath me.

⤎ 40 ⤏

I'M GETTING TOO NEAR THE SURFACE. LIGHT HURTS ME. TOO
much up there. I don't want to see. Letting myself sink again.
Can't see. I'm safer below.

What keeps bringing me up? Voices I like. By the time
I'm close enough to hear, they're gone. Danger. Dive again.
Dive down. Don't think about it. Deeper.

"Kilty? Kilty? Can you hear me? I'm here now. I love
you, Kilty."

"We all love you. We'll be back soon. Everything is fine.
We're all so glad you're safe."

Hands touch me. Gentle. I want to reply, but I'm too far
down now. Too hard to make it all the way up there again.

Soft hands on my forehead. Fragrance. I'm coming up
too fast. It hurts to come up. It hurts. "Anjang?" I moan.

"What did he say?"

"Could you understand him? It's a good sign, isn't it?"

But I'm going down again. All the way back down. It's
quiet down there. Tides wash over me. I rock softly in the
deep. Quiet. Deep.

There is an antiseptic smell. I know I'm at the surface again.
I can feel the light on the other side of my lids. Someone is

moving my arms and legs around. Everything is too dry. Sterile. I need soft green. I let myself sink again. But the sinking stops. Something keeps pulling me up to the surface. The air hurts me. Don't want to open my eyes.

Later it's dark. I can open my eyes now. A red light on one side. On the other a woman. I start. The light catches on her coppery hair. I moan.

"Kilty?" Very softly. A small hand touches my palm. She leans forward over me and brushes hair from my forehead.

"Kilty, it's me. Mom and Dad had to go back home, but I'm here. Can you hear me, Kilty? It's all right. You're safe. Everything's fine. You can go back to sleep if you want. I'll be here when you wake up. Don't worry. Don't worry now."

But I'm sinking again. It's better. Maybe I'll come back later.

It is bright daylight. I see a woman's back as she leaves through a green door. She wears white, blinding white. On the other side, a window with black bars. Everything is sharp, rigid, stiff. Beyond the bars there is mist and light.

When I come back again, someone is holding my hand. It is good. I let myself feel the touch of this good hand.

"Could you open the window?" My voice sounds funny, like I'm speaking from a long way away.

"Kilty!"

She is frightened. I can tell from her voice. I will have to open my eyes again. I hate to open my eyes. It's too sharp here. Too hard. Nevertheless, I open them. My sister Susanne is sitting next to the bed, holding my hand. I make a weak attempt at a smile.

"Can't talk yet. Open window, yes? Need good air." My God, I sound like a real goofus. Too bad. I'm sinking again. But before I am completely gone, I hear the sound of the window being pulled up and then—oh, delicious air, I smell delicious air. Fresh, cool damp. I groan with pleasure and surrender to the tide that is pulling me down again.

The next time I come to the surface, there are two men in the room. I keep my eyes closed. One asks the other when I can be questioned. His voice is urgent, and I feel his eyes on me even though mine are closed. The other voice says not for a few days certainly, as I have only spoken once. I hear him move, and a hand is laid protectively on my ankle. I want to stay and listen, but their voices keep blurring and I can't hold on any longer.

When I am back I open my eyes. Susanne is there. I can look into her warm brown eyes for a while. It's easy for me. "Window?" I say. But before it is open again I slide away.

I'm completely conscious. At least I think so. Something feels very different anyway. My eyes are closed, but a small hand is holding mine. I smile first.

"Kilty?" Her voice is soft.

"You got it." She laughs at my feeble joke. I roll my head slowly towards her and open my eyes. "Hi, beautiful."

Tears are rolling down her cheeks. She brushes them away. "Golly, I'm so dumb. I'm so sorry. You were reported missing, you know. We thought you were dead. It was so long, Kilty. I can't tell you what it was like. Then they called. They telephoned long distance and told us you'd been found. It's been like Christmas ever since."

I smiled. "Got to go. Back soon, okay?"

"Where are we?" My eyes are closed, but I know Susanne is there. I can feel her and smell her next to me.

Her hand rests on my arm. "Letterman Hospital in San Francisco. You've been here for eleven days. Before that you were in a hospital in China, I think. They won't tell us very much. It's all very hush, hush. We were told that you were picked up by the British in the jungle. You were delirious with fever, but the doctor says you're much better. I don't know what's going to happen. They just won't tell us much. But it's real nice here. The hospital staff is really fine. They let me sleep in a room down the hall if it's too late for me to go back to the boarding house where I'm staying. . . ." She hesitated. I was frowning. Something troubled me. I remembered.

"Bars?"

"Kilty, I just don't know much about it. This is a special room and there's someone from military intelligence outside all of the time. They think you know something important."

I rolled my head back and forth on the pillow. It was too much too think about. "See you, gorgeous." I was gone again.

❦ 41 ❦

I LIKE MY DOCTOR. HE'S CIVILIAN FOR SOME REASON, BUT A real nice guy. He'll hold the guys from M.I. off for another day or two. I can't quite figure out what they want me for, but it has something to do with my journal. I was found by the Brits, who airlifted me to one of their hospitals in China and from there I got sent home. Mom and Dad came down right away with Susanne from Eugene, but could only stay for a week. Susanne's here for a month anyway.

I'd like to take a look at my journal. Maybe I could figure out what's up. I was keeping a daily record from the time I left the main camp, after the explosion. Thought I could keep from going nuts if I wrote everyday, but maybe I wrote some crazy stuff. It was a crazy time. I guess I was in shock. Must have been.

I can't think about it yet. Too much I don't want to remember. I know I'll have to. But not yet.

Had my first meeting with the brass. Turns out it's my journal that's caused all the ruckus. All those mushroom-desolation dreams I so carefully recorded seem to scare the pants off them. I got my hands on the journal for a couple of minutes and read it out loud to them. But it's the pictures I drew that they're worried about. I guess towards the end when I was hallucinating I drew quite a few more pictures.

Just big mushrooms over desolate landscapes. I vaguely remember that I was consumed by the dream for a while. Plus I was completely out of my head.

Doctor Kent says I had both malaria and dengue fever, possibly at the same time. He doesn't know how I survived. I drank tea made from Anjang's herbs for a while, as long as they lasted anyway. I suspect that's what got me through the worst of it. I'm also filled with different kinds of strange parasites. But I'm here. I'm alive.

Colonel Norris said yesterday that they would release everything that was found with me except for my journal. Susanne's picking the stuff up for me today. They will all come back this afternoon for another hour of grilling, that's all Dr. Kent will allow. I certainly don't have anything to hide, but I can see that they don't believe my story. There are three of them: Norris is an Air Force full bird; there's the guy from military intelligence, and a third man who wasn't introduced to me, even though the other two defer to him when they're questioning me.

When they return today, they're bringing an anthropologist from Berkeley, an expert on native tribes from the area where they found me. They think he'll be able to verify the existence of the S'norra.

Susanne popped her head around the door, a big grin on her face. "I've got the package. I'm dying to see what you brought me from the jungle."

I'm kind of interested myself. I have almost no memory of a period of about a month. I know I built a crude hut when the fever starting getting really bad. There was the long period of the hellish dreams. Next thing I know I'm here. That's it.

She put a big package wrapped in brown paper and tied with string on the foot of the bed and started to work on the knots.

"Don't be too disappointed, okay?" I warned her. "It's probably just the clothes the Brits gave me to wear coming here."

"I don't think so, Kilty. The officer said it was the things that were found with you, with the exception of your journal."

She undid the last knot and carefully unfolded the rough paper. I watched her face. She reached inside, lifted something up, and then put it back, turning to me with a perplexed look on her face.

"What is it?"

She shook her head. "Not much. There's a piece of something, a blue rag or paper with red stains on it, and this"—she held up Uda's straight-edge razor—"and a garbage can lid."

My heart started beating so hard that I couldn't speak. I closed my eyes for a moment. I was starting to tremble. "Give it to me, Susanne." I managed to get the words out. "Please, give it to me."

Her eyes opened wide, and I could see fear on her face at something in my voice. She slid the parcel up where I could reach it. I pushed the paper down until I could see. The thunder beast. My loincloth. Uda's razor.

A terrible cry of pain escaped me when I saw them. I began to wail and scream. I reached over to the ashtray on my bedside table, filled with ashes and cigar butts from my visitors, and dumped the contents on my head, rubbing the ashes into my hair and down my face. I began to rock back and forth in my bed, wailing and moaning while the tears ran down my face.

"Kilty?" Her voice was shaking. "What's wrong? What can I do? What's the matter?"

209

I didn't, couldn't, answer her. I couldn't hold the memories off any longer. I remembered. I remembered it all. It was more than I could bear.

They shot me up with something, and it was a couple of days before I was coherent again. Susanne wouldn't let them take any of the things away. She even washed my loincloth and folded it in a drawer next to my bed. She's no dummy. She told me she had tried to keep the nurse from giving me the shot. "There's nothing wrong with crying, Kilty," she said. "But please don't dump the ashtray on your head again, okay?" She knew I wasn't nuts, and she's got a pretty remarkable sense of humor.

So I've got a couple of days to prepare before the colonel and his friends come again. I'll be ready. I know what I have to do now. I'm the messenger, after all. I even know what the message is. No problem.

Susanne is with me. I've asked her to drape my loincloth over the end of the bed where I can see it, and I've got the thunder beast hanging on the wall like a piece of art. I told her I had decorated the loincloth myself, and that it was a Stewart dress plaid. "Sure," she said.

Now everything is ready. She's sitting next to the bed with her steno pad and she tells me she can do a hundred and twenty words a minute. I'm going to deliver my message.

"It was just a milk run. We didn't expect any trouble. Hadn't been a Jap on this side of the mountains for days, so we didn't even have an escort. Then *Paper Doll* took the first hit. I thought we could make it back and had started the turn when we were hit again. I knew *Paper Doll* was going down."

✎ Author's Note ✎

ALTHOUGH THE S'NORRA TRIBE IS FICTIONAL, I HAVE USED
real-life sources for many of their techniques and traditions.

Like many others who value their own dreams, I first
learned about the Senoi dreamers of central Malaysia when I
read a short article by a young American anthropologist, Kilton
Stewart, reprinted in Charles Tart's *Altered States of Consciousness,* in 1972. Stewart's lyrical account of the Senoi, and in
particular, of their techniques for entering and transforming
dreams, confirmed my own belief that my dreams were more
significant than was generally believed, and that I could
actively use them to improve the quality of my waking life.

Stewart had been introduced to the Senoi by Herbert
Noone, a young British anthropologist and field ethnogra-
pher, who first discovered the tribe and their extraordinary
techniques in 1931. It was Herbert Noone who lived with the
Senoi, was adopted as a brother by a Senoi tribesman, and
who took a beautiful Senoi woman as a wife, although he did
not present her as such to his civilized colleagues. *In Search
of the Dream People,* written by Herbert Noone's brother,
Richard Noone, and Dennis Holman, vividly recounts the
story of Herbert Noone's adventures and eventual death in
the jungles of Malaysia in 1943.

It was also in 1972 that Patricia Garfield was inspired to
travel to Malaysia in search of the dream people, where she

211

successfully found and interviewed a number of tribe members who had survived the ravages of World War II on their country and culture. Garfield reported her findings in *Creative Dreaming*, her classic book on dreams, which was published in 1974.

I am indebted to Colin Turnbull's *The Forest People* for many of the details of daily life of the S'norra tribe. Turnbull's eloquent and touching account of the BaMbuti Pygmies of the Ituri Forest in the Congo is a book like no other, drawing the reader into a participatory experience of lives lived "in a world that is still kind and good. . . . And without evil."

I would also like to acknowledge Dorothy Bryant's exquisite fable, *The Kin of Ata Are Waiting for You,* a book I have used in dream workshops as an inspirational text since it was published by Moon Books in 1972. I have always assumed Bryant's book to be part of the network connecting Kilton Stewart's original nine and a half page article to dreamers everywhere, but I realize this is my own speculation.

The stories told by Uda, Masamo, and Anjang in *The Last of the Dream People* are strongly influenced by Jerome Rothenberg's translations of "primitive" and archaic poetry in *Technicians of the Sacred,* a text I strongly recommend to anyone who aspires to write. I am delighted to say that I have Rothenberg's permission to adapt and quote from his material.

I want to acknowledge the sources listed above with the deepest gratitude as they each have provided me with inspiration and delight for many years.

The flavor of the period surrounding World War II in my book is drawn directly from my own childhood memories.

In addition, I have found much that was helpful in the following books: James A. Michener's *Tales of the South Pacific*; Edward F. Murphy's *Heroes of WW II*; Mack Morris's *South Pacific Diary, 1942–1943*, edited by Ronnie Day; *A Flying Tiger's Diary* by Charles R. Bond, Jr., and Terry H. Anderson; *March to Victory*, edited by Tony Hall; and *The Road to Tokyo* by Keith Wheeler.

My thanks to Peter Michaud, Manager of the Bishop Museum Planetarium in Honolulu, for his help with constellation and star positions, and to my friend John Knoop, for his constant supply of enthusiastic encouragement and esoteric bits of information on World War II aircraft.

Thanks also to Peter Bloch and David Boatwright for sending me a copy of their beautiful original video of the Senoi tribe, filmed in Malaysia in 1974.

To Contact the Author

Alice Anne Parker conducts residential dream workshops and Reiki healing intensives at her home, a former Tibetan Buddhist retreat center on the windward side of the island of O'ahu, Hawaii.

If you would like information and a schedule of upcoming workshops, please write to her at: Buddha-Buddha, 53–086 Halai road, Hau'ula, HI 96717. Please include a stamped, self-addressed envelope for reply.

Additional Sources for Dream Work:
Dream Incubation Tapes

Dream incubation tapes offer a convenient and effective means of intensifying and directing your dreams. Each tape begins with a guided meditation, producing a body-relaxed, alert mind state. The tapes then guide you to create intense images and visions that lead to stimulating and memorable dreams. The original music accompanying the tapes was produced for the series by the internationally acclaimed composer Deuter.

Series I / Tape 1

Dream Clearing will unblock old images and recurrent dream patterns that may have been limiting your dream memory for years. (7:33 min.)

Dream Recall stimulates each sense with vivid images. The result is intense dream imagery and better recall of dreams. (8:39 min.)

Series I / Tape 2

Dream Guidance leads to a dream meeting with the aspect of yourself that can guide you comfortably and securely into knowledge of your own future. (8:41 min.)

Dream Healing offers guided imagery to enable you to visit Epidauros—healing center of the ancient world—to receive dreams that stimulate healing on an inner level. (8:41 min.)

Series I / Tape 3

Dream Exploration allows you to fly into dream adventures and explore other realms of consciousness while your body safely and comfortably sleeps. (10:55 min.)

The Black Velvet Room opens a dream world of sensuous pleasure and deep, refreshing sleep—an antidote to even the most stressful waking life. It can also be used as a remedy for insomnia. (9:56 min.)

Series II / Tape 1

Dreamsex lets you explore the depths of your own sexuality in the privacy and safety of the dream state. Opening the dream door to sexual fulfillment often leads to greater creative vitality in your waking life. (18:37 min.)

The Corridor of Dreams encourages dreams offering specific information about future projects—including their most likely outcome and barriers to success. (20:22 min.)

Series II / Tape 2

Dreamlover leads to a meeting in the dream state with your ideal other, to an aspect of self ready for integration, or to actual future lovers. (18:38 min.)

The Dark Vessel uses the classic imagery of setting out in a small boat across an expanse of dark water—originally created to lead the dreamer to contact with friends and relatives who are dead; it has also been valuable for terminally ill clients who wish to explore the after-death state in their dreams. (20:13 min.)

Order Form: Beyond Your Wildest Dreams:
Dream Incubation Tapes, Series I and II

All prices include postage and handling. For delivery outside the U.S., plase add an additional $2 per order.

Please send me:

Series #	Item description:	Price each	Total cost
Series I	All three tapes of Series I	$28.50	$_____
Series I	Dream Clearing/Dream Recall	$12.00	_____
Series I	Dream Guidance/Dream Healing	$12.00	_____
Series I	Dream Exploration/ Black Velvet Room	$12.00	_____
Series II	Both tapes of Series II	$22.50	_____
Series II	Dreamsex/Corridor of Dreams	$12.00	_____
Series II	Dreamlover/Dark Vessel (after-death state)	$12.00	_____

Enclosed payment of: $_____

Make check or money order payable to:
Real Dreams, 53–086 Halai Rd., Hau'ula, HI 96717

Method of payment: ___ check ___ money order
___ Visa ___ Mastercard

Credit Card Account Number: Expiration: Month Year

_____ ___ ___

Credit card orders must include a signature.

Signature: _____ Date: _____

Name: _____ (please print)

Address: _____

City: _____ State: _____ Zip: _____

Mail to: Real Dreams, 53–086 Halai Road, Hau'ula, HI 96717

ALSO FROM H J KRAMER

UNDERSTAND YOUR DREAMS:
1500 Dream Images and How to Interpret Them
by Alice Anne Parker

The essential guide to becoming your own dream expert—makes dreaming a pleasure and waking an adventure.

WAY OF THE PEACEFUL WARRIOR:
A Book That Changes Lives
by Dan Millman

A spiritual classic! The international best-seller that speaks directly to the universal quest for happiness.

SACRED JOURNEY OF THE PEACEFUL WARRIOR
by Dan Millman

The companion to the phenomenal story of the peaceful warrior's path to wisdom and harmony.

THE BLUE DOLPHIN:
A Parable by Robert Barnes

"A touching, warmhearted story in the spirit of *Jonathan Livingston Seagull*." —Dan Millman, author of *Way of the Peaceful Warrior*

If you are unable to find these books in your favorite bookstore, please call 800-833-9327.

ALSO FROM H J KRAMER

THE AWAKENED HEART:
Meditations on Finding Harmony
in a Changing World
by John Robbins and Anne Mortifee
An inquiry into the issues and concerns of the human heart.

TALKING WITH NATURE
by Michael J. Roads
The startling revelations of one man's
journey into the heart of nature's wisdom.

TARA'S ANGELS:
One Family's Extraordinary
Journey of Courage and Healing
by Kirk Moore
The singular account of a father's journey through grief
and the awakening of the soul of a family to profound
love and spiritual purpose.

RESTORING THE EARTH:
Visionary Solutions From the Bioneers
by Kenny Ausubel
Offering practical solutions for virtually all our
crucial environmental problems, these working
models hold keys to planetary survival.

If you are unable to find these books in your favorite
bookstore, please call 800-833-9327.